DESTINATION NEW YORK

Quebec
St. Lawrence River
CANADA
N
W
E
S
CANADA
UNITED STATES
MEXICO
Ontario
UNITED STATES
VT
Lake Ontario
New York
Albany
MA
Lake Erie
Hudson River
CT
Long Island Sound
Long Island
New York
Sandy Hook
Pennsylvania
New Jersey
Legend
Port City
0 40 80 miles
0 40 80 kilometers
ATLANTIC OCEAN

DESTINATION NEW YORK

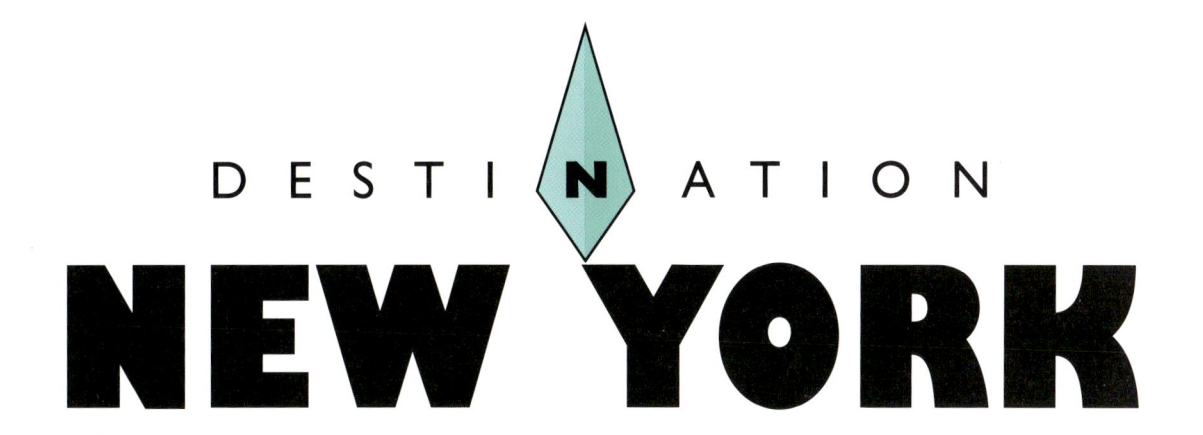

by Linda Tagliaferro

Lerner Publications Company • Minneapolis

PHOTO ACKNOWLEDGMENTS
Cover photo by © Betty Crowell. All inside photos courtesy of: © Tony Lagruth, pp. 5, 28, 48, 54; Port Authority of New York and New Jersey, pp. 6, 16, 17, 19, 20 (top and bottom), 45, 52; © James Marshall, pp. 9, 24, 46, 47, 66 (middle), 67, 73 (top right), 76; © Carol Kitman, pp. 10 (top), 11, 68 (bottom), 73 (left); New York State Department of Economic Development, pp. 10 (bottom), 71, 74-75; © Richard B. Levine, pp. 15, 26, 53, 62, 66 (top and bottom), 70; © Linda Tagliaferro, pp. 18, 51, 55; © David Sailors, pp. 23, 27, 57; Library of Congress, pp. 31, 32, 43 (bottom), 44; J. Clarence Davies Collection, Museum of the City of New York, pp. 34-35; Archive Photos, pp. 35 (bottom), 37, 40, 43 (top); Corbis-Bettmann, p. 39; Historic Urban Plans, p. 41; Museum of the City of New York/Archive Photos, p. 43 (top); © Frances M. Roberts, pp. 60-61, 68 (top); M. Bryan Ginsberg, p. 69; Steve Eisenberg, p. 80. Maps by Ortelius Design.

To the memory of my grandparents, Giuseppa and Vincenzo Ciulla and Lorenza and Vincenzo Tagliaferro, whose journeys through Ellis Island from southern Italy made it possible for me to be born in New York, the most exciting city in the world.

Copyright © 1998 by Linda Tagliaferro

All rights reserved. International copyright secured. No part of this book may be reproduced, stored in a retrieval system, or transmitted in any form or by any means—electronic, mechanical, photocopying, recording, or otherwise—without prior written permission of Lerner Publications Company, except for the inclusion of brief quotations in an acknowledged review.

Website address: www.lernerbooks.com

LIBRARY OF CONGRESS CATALOGING-IN-PUBLICATION DATA

Tagliaferro, Linda.
    Destination New York / by Linda Tagliaferro
      p. cm. — (Port cities of North America)
    Includes index.
    Summary: An introduction to the port city of New York, describing its geography, history, economy, and daily life.
      ISBN 0-8225-2793-6 (lib. bdg. : alk. paper)
    1. New York (N.Y.)—Juvenile literature. [1. New York (N.Y.)]
I. Title. II. Series.
F128.33.T34 1998
974.7'1—dc21   97–10570

Manufactured in the United States of America
1 2 3 4 5 6 – JR – 03 02 01 00 99 98

The glossary that begins on page 76 gives definitions of words shown in **bold type** in the text.

CONTENTS

CHAPTER ONE	The Great Harbor	7
CHAPTER TWO	From Beaver Skins to Big Business	29
CHAPTER THREE	Give and Take	49
CHAPTER FOUR	The Big Apple	63
	Glossary	76
	Pronunciation Guide	77
	Index	78
	About the Author	80

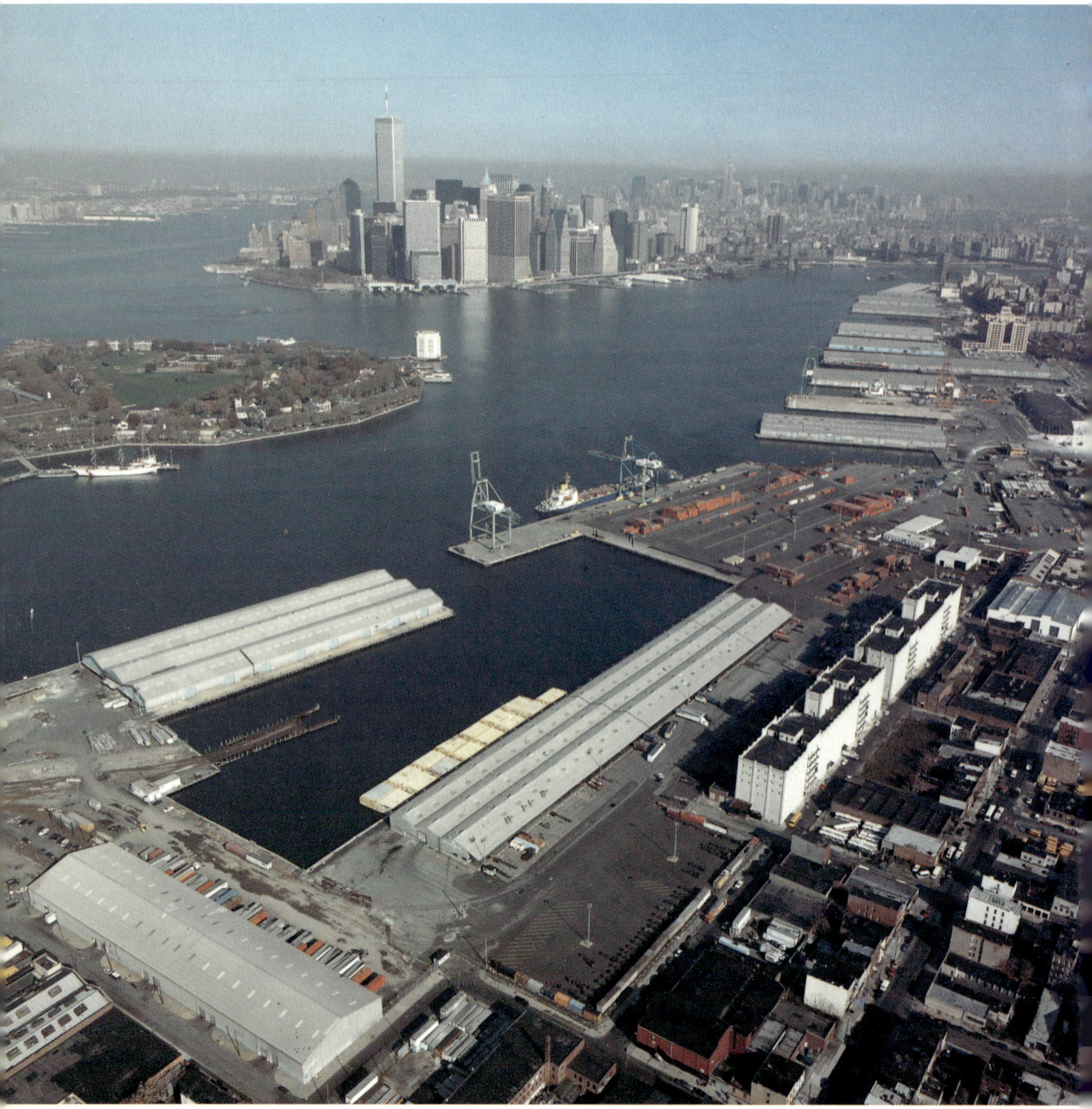

CHAPTER ONE

THE GREAT HARBOR

New York City's naturally deep harbor and modern facilities (facing page) *make it one of the top-ranked ports in the United States.*

More than one million years ago, a tremendous event changed the face of North America and resulted in the birth of the land that is known as New York City. A huge glacier, or river of ice, taller than the skyscrapers that now fill Manhattan, covered most of the Northern Hemisphere. The glacier moved under its own immense weight and crept slowly across the continent, eventually stopping in the vicinity of what is now New York. Along the way, the glacier carved out huge expanses such as the Hudson River Valley. When the global climate gradually changed from frigid to warm, the enormous glacier retreated. As the ice melted, water rushed in to fill the deep depressions carved by the glacier. Most of what became New York City settled firmly in its present location as a group of land masses connected underwater but separated on the surface by rivers and bays. Nature had masterfully created one of the finest natural harbors in the world.

A City of Islands

There is only one New York City, but it is not all located on one piece of land. The number one seaport on the East Coast of the United States is made up physically of different parts, and some of these parts are separate islands. The city's urban isles are so well connected by a massive network of bridges, tunnels, and ferries that even native New Yorkers sometimes forget that they live on land masses surrounded by rivers and bays.

New York City is located in the southeastern corner of the state of New York. Vermont, Massachusetts, and Connecticut border New York to the east, while Pennsylvania and New Jersey lie to the south. Lakes Erie and Ontario run along the western border of New York. The St. Lawrence Seaway separates the state from the Canadian province of Quebec. The modern seaport city covers 301 square miles and is divided into five boroughs (or parts)—Manhattan, Queens, Brooklyn, the Bronx, and Staten Island.

The island of Manhattan is 13.4 miles long and 2.3 miles wide. A 16-mile-long tidal **strait** known as the East River separates Manhattan from Brooklyn and Queens to the east. Although these two boroughs are politically and

The borough of Manhattan is known for its towering buildings and famous skyline.

culturally part of New York City, they physically make up the western portion of Long Island, which stretches out over 100 miles and is shaped like an enormous fish. To the north of Long Island is a waterway called Long Island Sound, which connects to New York Harbor via the East River.

Located on the southern tip of New York, the Bronx is the only borough that is on the U.S. mainland. The Bronx is separated from Manhattan to the south by the Harlem River and by Spuyten Duyvil Creek. Staten Island lies to the southwest of Manhattan, across Upper New York Bay. The Hudson River runs along the West Side of Manhattan and separates the borough from the state of New Jersey. Two channels, the Arthur Kill and the Kill Van Kull, divide Staten

9

Island from New Jersey. In addition to the five boroughs, three islands—Governor's Island, Liberty Island, and Ellis Island—are located in Upper New York Bay.

Although different bodies of water separate the boroughs, a number of bridges and tunnels allow people to get from one area to another. The famous Brooklyn Bridge connects Manhattan and Brooklyn, while the Triborough Bridge links Manhattan, Queens, and the Bronx. The Verrazano-Narrows Bridge, one of the longest suspension bridges in the world, connects Staten Island with Brooklyn. In addition, the Lincoln Tunnel, the Holland Tunnel, and the George Washington Bridge provide quick access from Manhattan to New Jersey. Because many people who work in Manhattan live in other boroughs or in New Jersey, bridges and tunnels are a vital part of daily life.

The Brooklyn Bridge (above) and the Staten Island Ferry (left) help New Yorkers get from one borough to another. Because the city includes 65 square miles of inland water, bridges and ferries are crucial to the local transportation network.

A cargo vessel sails through New York Harbor. More than 4,500 ships visit the Port of New York and New Jersey each year.

Size of the Port ➤ The word "port" comes from the Latin *portus,* which means "gate." New York City is truly a gateway to the United States, offering a convenient, sheltered harbor to ships coming to the United States from around the world via the Atlantic Ocean. The total area of the actual port is 1,500 square miles, all within a 25-mile radius of the Statue of Liberty, the renowned monument that has welcomed millions of immigrants to a new life in America. The port has 755 miles of shoreline. Of this expanse, 460 miles lie on the New York side of the Hudson River, and the other 295 miles lie on the New Jersey side of the river. As a result, the port is known as the Port of New York and New Jersey.

New York Harbor, which forms the main entrance to the port, is composed of Upper New York Bay and Lower New York Bay. These two bodies of water are connected by a strait called the Narrows, which runs between Brooklyn and Staten Island. Water from the Hudson River, the East River, and the Kill Van Kull converges in the Upper Bay, which covers an area from the Narrows to the tip of Manhattan Island. The Lower Bay stretches south from the Narrows and into the Atlantic Ocean. Sandy Hook, a **spit** off the coast of New Jersey, marks the entrance to the Lower Bay for incoming ships.

The Port of New York and New Jersey has many natural advantages that led to its development as a thriving center of trade. The proximity of the port to the open ocean helps cut down on shipping time. The harbor's deep channels and the shelter it offers from strong ocean winds make the port popular for incoming ships. In addition, the harbor's current, or movement of the water, is strong. The constant movement of water prevents ice from forming in the harbor, even though New York City winters can be severe.

> ▶ Hell Gate is a segment of the East River known for its turbulent, swirling waters—which were the cause of many historical shipwrecks. Hell Gate was given its name by early Dutch settlers.
>
> ▶ The Hudson River is 306 miles long and runs south from the Catskill Mountains in upstate New York to New York City.

One Port in Two States

At one time, all of the port's facilities were located in Manhattan. In the late 1950s, however, new technologies had a tremendous impact on shipping. The shift towards a new method of loading and unloading cargo, called **containerization,** caused the port to expand to the nearby shores of New Jersey. The relatively uncrowded areas across the Hudson River provided the extra open spaces needed for the storage of goods that are shipped in the 20-foot or 40-foot rectangular steel boxes known as containers. Since the 1950s, a great deal of the transfer of merchandise has taken place in New Jersey.

13

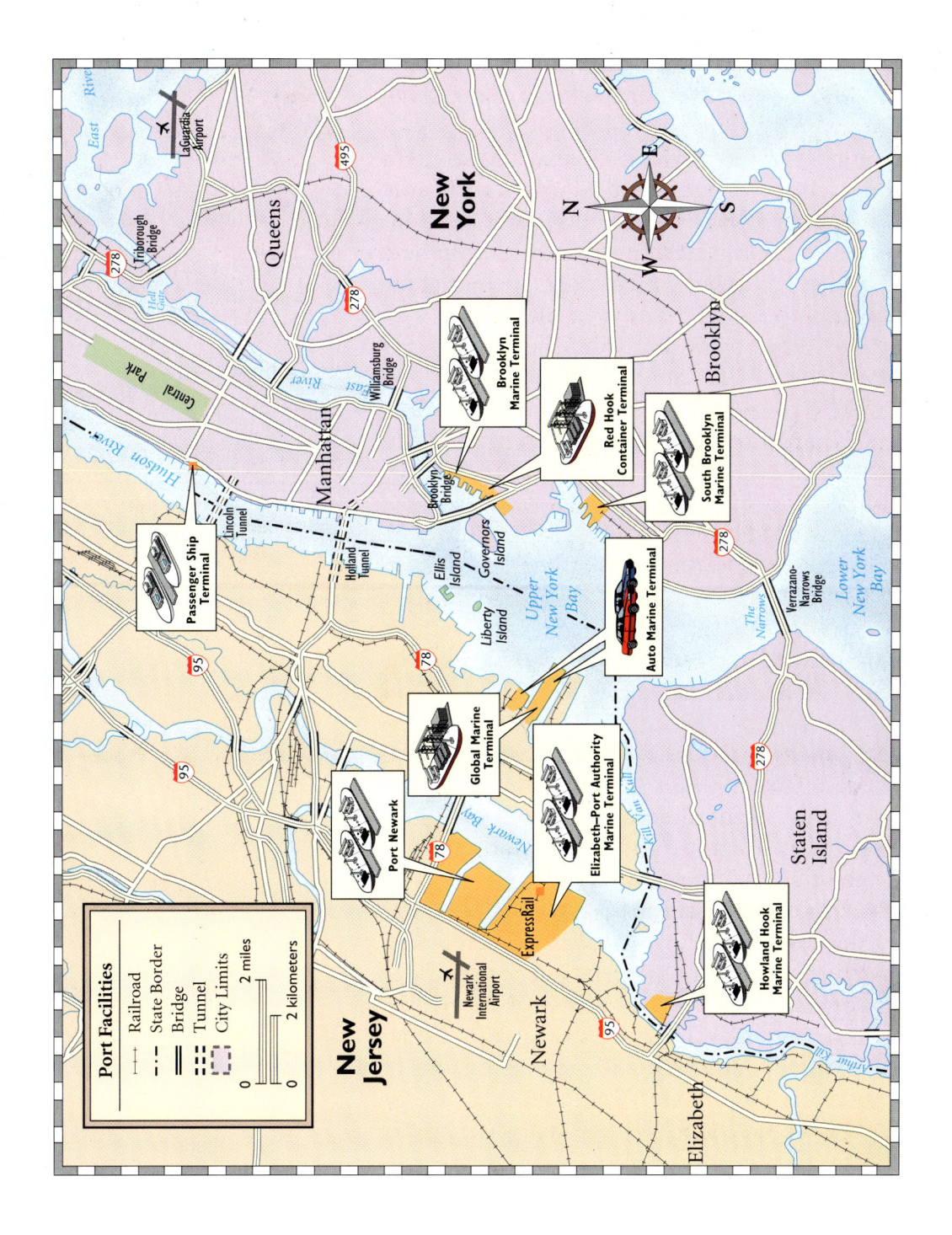

Federal, state, and local government agencies are responsible for monitoring port activity. These agencies include the U.S. Army Corps of Engineers, the U.S. Coast Guard, and the Port Authority of New York and New Jersey. Created in 1921, the Port Authority has promoted commerce in the bistate port and made improvements within the shared harbor. These include the construction of bridges and tunnels as well as the upgrading of port facilities.

Types of Cargo

Containerization is the most important form of maritime trade. Shippers use containers to move a variety of items, from electronic goods to clothing to bananas. Perishable cargo is transported in refrigerated containers. Shipping companies like containers because they ensure safe handling and protect goods from harsh weather and vandalism. Since the advent of containerization, New York Harbor has been a major destination for container cargo. The Port of New York and New Jersey is among the top 15 container ports in the world and is the third largest container port in North America. The port moves more than two million **TEUs** (twenty-foot equivalent units) of container cargo each year.

Besides handling containers, the port is also equipped to move dry **bulk cargo** such as salt, sand, or grains. Bulk products are not packaged but are loaded directly onto ships by conveyor belts or other machinery. The port also handles liquid bulk products such as orange juice concentrate, vegetable oil, and petroleum. More than 36 million long tons of bulk cargo moved through the port in 1996.

A colorful stack of containers awaits shipment at the Red Hook Container Terminal, operated by the American Stevedoring Company. The standard size of a shipping container is 20 feet by 8 feet.

▶ The Port of New York and New Jersey measures cargo in long tons. One long ton equals 2,240 pounds.

▶ The Port of New York and New Jersey handles more general cargo than any other port on the East Coast of the United States.

▶ Bulk products made up 72 percent of the port's total oceanborne trade in 1996, while general cargo accounted for 28 percent of the total trade.

Certain commodities that come into the port are packaged in separate units such as boxes, bags, or pallets. For instance, coffee beans are shipped in large sacks that weigh more than 100 pounds. Items shipped in this manner are known as **breakbulk cargo,** which can also refer to products, such as lumber or heavy machinery, that are too large to be placed in containers. Container and breakbulk goods fall into the category of **general cargo.** The port handled more than 14 million long tons of general cargo in 1996.

Moving cargo on and off ships involves port workers called longshoremen and all kinds of motorized equipment. **Gantry cranes,** which move containers and other heavy items, are one of the most visible types of equipment at the port. These cranes weigh anywhere from 700 to 1,000 tons and can tower as high as a 20-storied building. Gantry-crane operators sit high up on the crane in an enclosure called the operator's cab, which moves on a track and has windows with a view of the surrounding docks and the ships below. From the cab, the operator directs the movement of the immense crane up and down the dock and on board the ships that are to be loaded and unloaded.

Gantry cranes at the Howland Hook Marine Terminal in Staten Island lift containers from a docked ship. Container cargo can be loaded and unloaded much more quickly than breakbulk goods.

Containers are constructed with square holes in each corner. The crane operator picks up the containers by inserting the pins of the crane's spreader, which look like pointed arrowheads, into the square holes, then twisting and locking the pins into place. The containers can then be moved to and from the ships. Floating, mobile cranes are also available at the port to assist the movement of heavy and oversized breakbulk cargo.

Port Facilities ▶ Business is big at the number-one port on the East Coast. Port Newark and the Elizabeth-Port Authority Marine Terminal, both located in Newark Bay on the New Jersey side of the port, handle more than 12 million long tons of container cargo every year. Together they are the most active container terminal on the East Coast of the United States. This complex, which is called the Port Newark/Elizabeth Marine Terminal, also forms the largest and most versatile terminal in the port. The complex includes container-handling terminals, automobile

The Port Newark/Elizabeth Marine Terminal houses five container terminals that together offer shippers 17,000 feet of berth space and 30 gantry cranes.

17

processing and storage facilities, liquid and solid bulk terminals, and breakbulk facilities. The Port Newark/Elizabeth Marine Terminal also has more than 5.5 million square feet of warehouse space for storing cargo as large as cars or as small as coffee beans.

The Auto Marine Terminal in Bayonne, New Jersey, is a **dedicated wharf** that specializes in the handling of foreign and domestic automobiles. Cars and other vehicles are shipped to the port in roll-on/roll-off vessels. Vehicles drive directly on and off ro-ro ships through openings in the side or stern (rear) of the ship instead of being lifted off by cranes. Longshoremen wear special coveralls and gloves to keep new vehicles clean as they drive them on or off the ships. Located adjacent to this terminal is the Global Marine Terminal, which is designed for container service and is the only privately owned terminal in the port.

On the New York side of the port, shipping activity is centered in the borough of Brooklyn. Facilities include the Red Hook Container Terminal, the Brooklyn Marine Terminal, and the South Brooklyn Marine Terminal. The 80-acre Red Hook Terminal has some of the most up-to-date facilities in the port and can handle container, breakbulk, and ro-ro cargo. The Brooklyn Marine Terminal, located next to Red Hook, consists of three piers that are used for loading, unloading, and warehousing breakbulk goods. The piers at South Brooklyn Marine Terminal also handle breakbulk and ro-ro cargo and have 600,000 square feet of storage space.

Staten Island is home to the Howland Hook Marine Terminal, which is owned by the city of

With the World Trade Center in the background, an onboard crane unloads sacks of cacao beans, a form of breakbulk cargo.

Port workers drive new cars off a ro-ro ship at the Auto Marine Terminal, which was designed to handle automobile imports and exports.

New York and leased to the Port Authority. The terminal is designed for high-volume container operations, with 2,500 feet of berth space and seven gantry cranes. The only remaining terminal in Manhattan is the New York City Passenger Ship Terminal, located on the Hudson River. Cruises departing from the terminal sail to the Caribbean islands, Bermuda, Europe, and the Canadian Maritime Provinces, which include New Brunswick, Nova Scotia, and Prince Edward Island. In 1996 nearly 400,000 passengers passed through the terminal.

Quick Connections ▶ One important advantage that the port offers is its accessibility to the rest of the United States and Canada. Goods arriving from foreign ports can be forwarded conveniently to inland

19

The port's extensive road and rail connections enable cargo to be moved quickly and efficiently to other parts of the country. At the ExpressRail facility (above), containers are stacked onto railroad cars for delivery to market. Gantry cranes also load containers onto flatbed trucks (left), which carry the cargo to market or to train yards to be transferred onto railroad cars.

20

markets in a variety of ways. All of the port terminals have connections to four interstate highways and a number of expressways that provide efficient routes for sending goods farther inland by truck. One example is I-95—the New Jersey Turnpike—which becomes the New England Thruway farther north and connects to Boston, Massachusetts, and to other cities in New England. I-95 also leads south and continues down the East Coast to Florida.

The movement of freight by more than one form of transport in the course of a single trip is known as **intermodal transportation.** Containers, which are designed to ride on truck trailers and railroad flatcars, have simplified this process. To help move goods to and from inland markets, 14 intermodal train yards lie within the vicinity of the Port of New York and New Jersey. Because rail transport is cheaper than trucking, trains are often used to haul containers and other goods over long distances.

Rail service is carried out primarily by regional railroads such as Conrail, as well as by the New York, Susquehanna and Western Railway. The Delaware Hudson Railway, which is run by Canadian Pacific rail services, also serves the port. While many of the train yards are located away from the port, some terminals have dockside rail service, which facilitates the transfer of containers. With on-dock rail, container cargo can be placed directly onto a train and delivered to its destination. ExpressRail and the Marine On-Dock Auto Rail Terminal (MODART) are two facilities that offer dockside rail service.

Three major airports—John F. Kennedy International Airport and LaGuardia Airport in

> ➤ With easy access to highways and train tracks, goods can be shipped quickly and efficiently from the port to such major U.S. cities as Minneapolis, Atlanta, Dallas, Chicago, and Seattle.
>
> ➤ More than 10,000 trucking companies conduct business with the Port of New York and New Jersey.

Queens and Newark International Airport in New Jersey—serve the port. The three airports combined handle more air cargo than any other system of airports in the entire world. These airports, which form the largest regional airport complex in the country, also send more than 70 million passengers each year to domestic and international destinations.

Ships traveling from the eastern shores of the Atlantic may take a week to arrive at the Port of New York and New Jersey. Toward the end of the ocean journey, welcoming sights will be seen from the incoming ship. At first, the ship's radar picks up the presence of land as far away as 27 miles offshore. About 15 miles from the Verrazano-Narrows Bridge, the ship will reach the Ambrose Light Tower. This large structure off the coast of Sandy Hook, New Jersey, sends out a flashing light that can be seen as far away as 20 miles and helps guide vessels toward the harbor entrance. Approaching ever closer, the crew will see land from about 9 miles away.

Once the ship arrives at the Ambrose Light Tower, the Sandy Hook Pilots send out one of their pilots in a small boat to meet the incoming vessel. The boat lines up alongside the larger ship, whose crew members provide what is called a Jacob's ladder. The crew members throw this ladder—which is made of rope—over the side of the ship, where it dangles about three feet above the surface of the water. The experienced pilot jumps up to catch the ladder and climbs 60 or 70 feet, sometimes in inclement weather, to board the ship. The pilot then navigates the ship into the harbor. Although the

◄ Arriving at the Port

> ► A U.S. Coast Guard officer describes the Ambrose Light Tower as looking like "a huge chair in the middle of the water."

captain of the arriving ship is an experienced navigator, he or she may not be familiar with all the different features of this port.

In order to qualify as a Sandy Hook pilot, applicants must take a demanding test, which includes drawing the entire harbor from memory. The aspiring pilot must know the varying depths of the harbor, as well as the location of shoals—sandy elevations at the bottom of the harbor—that can pose a threat to navigation. Not knowing all these details could lead to a disaster.

As the incoming ship sails through the Ambrose Channel in the Lower Bay, the pilot relies on lights and buoys to guide the vessel through the Narrows and into the Upper Bay. The ship is then directed to one of the port's many terminals, where the cargo is awaited.

After an incoming vessel has navigated through the Narrows and into Upper New York Bay, the crew will catch sight of New York City's familiar skyline.

A tugboat pulls a fully loaded container barge across New York Harbor. The port's cross-harbor barge service delivers cargo between Red Hook Container Terminal in Brooklyn and marine terminals in New Jersey.

Trade Creates Traffic

More than 1,000 vessels cross New York Harbor every day. These include the tugboats that guide large cargo vessels in and out of docking spaces, ferries that provide service for commuters traveling between boroughs, pleasure craft, and numerous barges. To ensure the safety of all these vessels, the U.S. Coast Guard's Vessel Traffic Services is in charge of monitoring the marine traffic in the port. From its headquarters on Staten Island, the Coast Guard operates radar sites on Governor's Island and 12 additional locations that run from Sandy Hook throughout the Lower Bay.

Radar—electronic equipment that sends out radio beams from ships or radar stations—facilitates the navigation of oceans and harbors. Radar beams bounce off other ships or land masses, and when the signals return to the original radar screen, they provide an electronic picture of what lies in the surroundings, even during fogs or storms. Most modern ships have their own radar system, which enables pilots to track other ships' positions. Pilots can communicate their movements to other vessels via radio. An international law requires that an English-speaking person be on board at all times.

Twenty-four hours before a vessel enters the harbor, the shipping agent—who represents the owner of the vessel at the port—must notify the Coast Guard of the ship's arrival. Coast Guard officers must be told exactly where the vessel is heading. In addition, the agent must notify the Coast Guard of any special risks, so that precautions can be taken when directing a vessel through harbor waters. Every few months a high-risk vessel, such as a ship carrying butane gas, may enter the harbor. If a ship loaded with gas were to collide with another vessel, it could blow up and cause an explosion covering an area of 12 miles.

Luckily, the port faces few such risks. Most often heating oil and petroleum products come into the port by barge. The tankers that transport gas and other petroleum products overseas often have very deep drafts, which means that a large amount of the ship lies below the water line. Deep drafts make it impossible for tankers to travel through the shallow waters that lead to refineries located along the coast of New Jersey. Instead, the tankers sail to deep anchorages (holding areas) in the Narrows, where they unload their fuel onto barges. These flat-bottomed boats are much more maneuverable than the large tankers and can transport a variety of cargoes along the shallow inland waterways.

THE DREDGING QUESTION

When the current of the Hudson River flushes sediment from Albany, New York, southward toward the port, it creates a buildup at the bottom of New York Harbor. This buildup makes the water shallower. To maintain the harbor depth, special boats called dredges scoop up mud and rock from the bottom of the harbor and dump the sediment into an onboard tank or onto a barge alongside the dredge. The material is later deposited at a dump site.

Dredging has long been a subject of debate at the port. The harbor's water depth varies from 35 to 40 feet. The advent of larger ships requires the port to maintain deeper navigational channels. This has posed an economic problem for the port. Some people worry that if the harbor is not deepened regularly, shippers will reroute their vessels to deeper harbors, and the port will lose money.

However, some environmentalists are concerned that continued dredging could pose a threat to the marine environment, because much of the sediment has been contaminated by sewage dumped into the harbor by local chemical industries. Previously, barges transported this toxic waste to an area in the Atlantic Ocean six miles east of Sandy Hook, New Jersey, known as the Mud Dump Site. This location was overused, and officials closed it in 1997. Some proposed alternatives have been artificial islands or underwater pits that could be sealed after toxic sediment was buried there. As of yet, no one solution has been chosen. For the port to survive and prosper, future solutions to the dredging problem will have to strike a balance between economic and environmental concerns.

Environmental Concerns ▶ The Coast Guard is vigilant in managing the port's ecological issues. One of their duties is to protect environmentally sensitive areas such as Arthur Kill in Staten Island. This area provides nesting grounds for waterfowl and supports grasses and reeds that are commonly found in wetlands. The Coast Guard has maps of especially sensitive areas and takes precautions to avoid oil spills and other ecological disasters that could kill animals and plants and pollute the water.

The Coast Guard is also responsible for establishing regulations governing the construction of oil tankers and other ships that carry polluting substances into U.S. ports. One example of such regulations is the Ocean Pollution Act of 1990, which requires tankers to have double hulls by the beginning of the twenty-first century. A leak in a double-hull ship would fall into the lower hull of the vessel rather than into the water. In addition, the Ocean Pollution Act prevents small oil spills that occur when ships unload oil into dockside storage tanks.

Since its very beginnings, the port has faced environmental challenges such as these, but its ability to adapt will enable it to continue to thrive as a safe, productive center for trade during changing times.

Along the Arthur Kill, which runs between New Jersey and Staten Island, workers have planted smooth chord grass to help restore wetlands that provide a habitat for different kinds of plants and animals. The U.S. Coast Guard is responsible for protecting such environmentally sensitive areas.

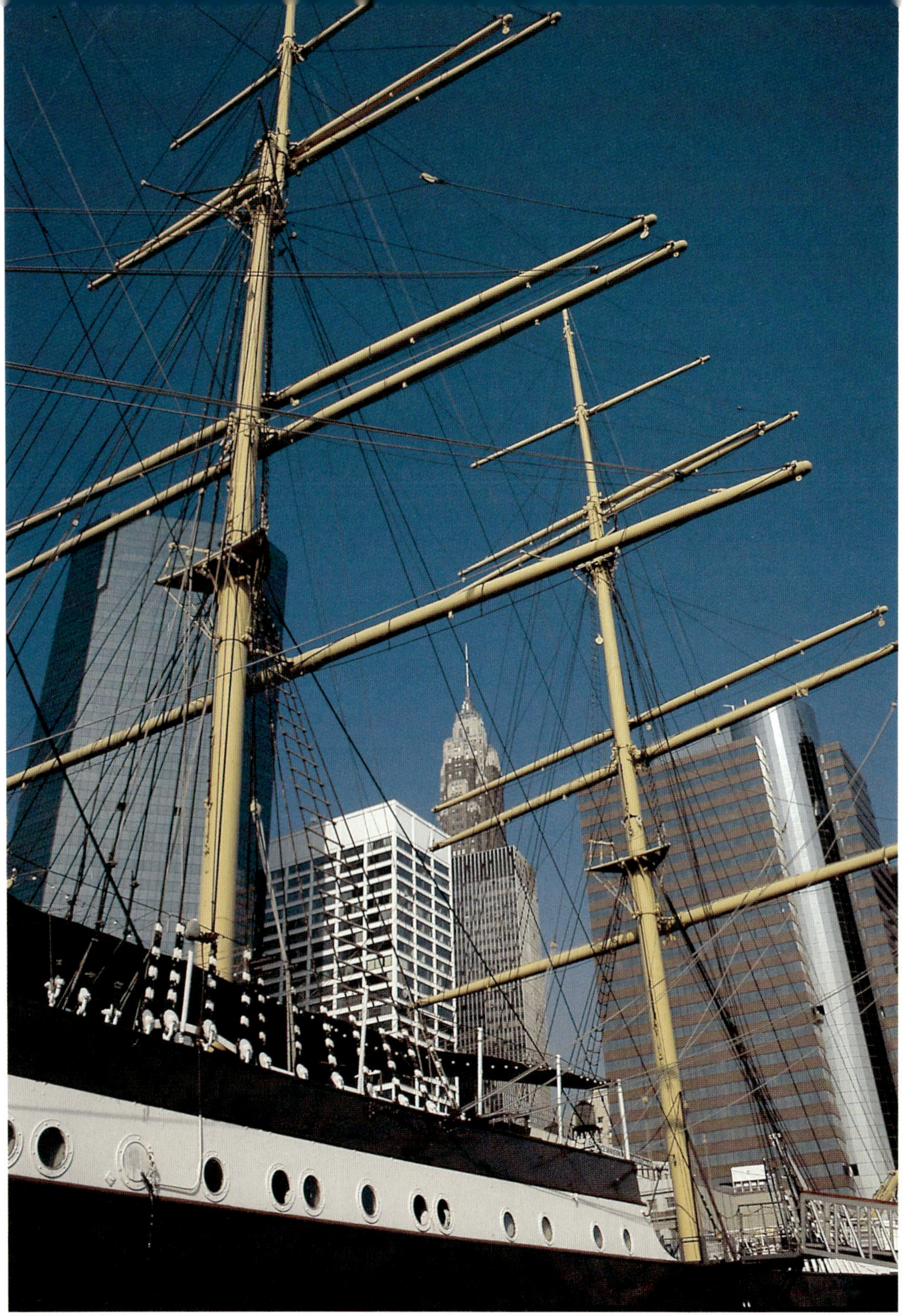

CHAPTER TWO

FROM BEAVER SKINS TO BIG BUSINESS

Historic ships at the South Street Seaport (facing page) *remind New Yorkers of the port's role in the development of the city.*

Long before the World Trade Center, the Statue of Liberty, or the Staten Island Ferry existed, the island of Manhattan was covered with forests and filled with wildlife. Surrounding waters were abundant with marine animals. More than 11,000 years ago, after the glaciers that once covered the region had melted, the first inhabitants of what is now Manhattan Island came to the area in search of food. These Indian groups were the descendants of the peoples who had earlier migrated from Asia by crossing a land bridge near the present-day Bering Strait. Pursuing large game and other sources of food, these people slowly made their way across what are now Canada and the United States.

The paleo-Indians who came to Manhattan Island hunted animals such as elk and caribou and gathered wild-growing plants. When they reached the island, they were greatly rewarded for their efforts to find food. Bears, wolves, and deer roamed free. The island was also inhabited by wild turkeys, red and gray foxes, weasels, and mink. The Indians ceased their search, settled in the area, and reaped the benefits of this hunting paradise.

The Lenape

Eventually a group that called themselves the Lenape—also known as the Delaware Indians by later European settlers—arrived in the area of Manhattan Island. The many subdivisions of this Indian nation spoke Munsee, Unami, and other dialects of a language belonging to the large Algonquian language family. The Lenape lived in small villages consisting of bark- and grass-covered huts built close to the shore. They traveled along the region's waterways in dugout canoes that they had carved out of huge trees. These canoes could carry as many as 12 people per vessel.

The Lenape traveled in their canoes to hunt, fish, and trade with other Native peoples in the area. Although the coastal area they inhabited provided all the necessities of life, trade was a significant part of the Lenape lifestyle. An important trade item was seashells, which the Lenape used to make wampum. The Lenape used wampum—purple and white seashells strung together like beads—for sacred rituals and as a form of money.

Europeans Arrive ▶ In 1524 Giovanni da Verrazano, an Italian explorer who worked for King Francis I of France, sailed into the Lower Bay, seeking a westward passage to Asia. Other Europeans followed Verrazano's path across the Atlantic Ocean. One such explorer was Henry Hudson, an English sailor who was employed by the Dutch. In 1609 he set sail in his vessel, the *Half Moon,* and arrived at the river that was later named after him.

Although Hudson was also searching for a route to Asia, he accidentally found something more valuable—an excellent natural harbor with different types of riches. He soon realized that the Indians were willing to trade beaver, otter, mink, and other animal pelts (skins) for manufactured objects such as hatchets and beads.

On his third attempt to find a northern sea route to Asia, Henry Hudson changed course and landed his ship along the East Coast of North America. From there he traveled up what would become the Hudson River all the way to present-day Albany. While in New York Harbor, Hudson and his crew exchanged gifts with local Native peoples.

The animal skins were plentiful in the newly explored land and could fetch high prices in Europe, where beaver hats and other items made of fur were quite popular.

Shortly after Hudson's voyage, Dutch merchants commissioned two adventurers from their country, Adriaen Block and Hendrik Christiaensen, to sail into the inviting harbor and to explore the regions that Hudson had visited. After successfully trading with the Indians, they returned to their native Holland with a large cargo of furs, and the Dutch realized the financial potential of this new trade. On a second voyage in the winter of 1613–14, one of Block's ships caught fire while anchored in the harbor. Using the rich timber in the area, Block's crew built a new ship, the *Onrust,* which means "restless" in the Dutch language. This started a shipbuilding tradition in the area.

By 1621 the government in Holland had granted permission to a business called the Dutch West India Company to engage in trade in the lands lying between the Hudson River, which the Dutch called the North River, and the Delaware River, which they referred to as the South River. The company called the province New Netherland. The Dutch province included parts of present-day New York, New Jersey, Delaware, and Connecticut. In 1624 the Dutch West India Company sent 30 families on a ship to the new province and provided them with cattle, farming tools, and other supplies that would allow them to set up a colony.

By 1626 the Dutch had founded a permanent settlement on the southern tip of Manhattan Island. The small town was known as New Am-

Although trade between the Lenape and the European settlers initially thrived, relations deteriorated when the Indians realized that the newcomers wanted to displace them.

sterdam, in honor of the capital of Holland, and it consisted of a fort and houses built along the East River. The colonists of New Amsterdam learned to harvest both the bounty of the surrounding waters as well as the fruits of their own crops, including the corn and squash that the Lenape taught them to cultivate.

Peter Minuit became the first governor of New Amsterdam in 1626, and he is said to have bought Manhattan Island from the Lenape residents in exchange for 60 Dutch guilders' worth (about $24) of assorted objects, such as beads and knives. Some people doubt whether this deal was fair, because it probably meant different things to the Lenape and to the Dutch. The Lenape had no concept of the ownership of nature and may have thought they were merely agreeing to share the land with the Europeans. Others wonder whether this transaction really occurred, and if it did, whether the Indians involved in the transaction actually lived on the island.

Dealings with the Dutch brought more than trade to the Lenape. The European newcomers also brought alcohol and firearms, as well as previously unknown diseases such as smallpox and measles. Deadly epidemics broke out among the Indians because they had no natural immunity to these foreign sicknesses. In addition, conflicts occasionally erupted between the Dutch and the Indians. As the colony became more established, the settlers slowly forced the Lenape out of the area.

The Seaport's Beginnings ▶ In 1648 Peter Stuyvesant became the governor of New Amsterdam. The colony was growing at

By the 1650s, New Amsterdam had grown into an established colony and a center of trade. The commerce-minded Dutch took advantage of the city's deepwater harbor, which could accommodate large ships carrying supplies and trade items.

this time, as settlers began to move into the areas that became New York's outer boroughs. In 1648 workers built the first wharf on the East River. In the following year, a second wharf was built, and New Amsterdam was on its way to becoming the greatest seaport in the world. The new city developed a flour trade with German farms in what is now upstate New York. These farmers produced flour that was shipped through the port to the Caribbean. In those warm islands, merchants traded the flour for sugar, which was in turn shipped to Europe.

By this time, the Dutch colony was surrounded by English colonies in New England and on the eastern end of Long Island. Although the Dutch West India Company had assumed the rights to all the land between the Delaware River and Cape Cod in Massachusetts, the English never recognized this claim. In 1664 King Charles II of England decided to give his brother, James, the Duke of York, some special gifts. These gifts included the land that the Dutch claimed as New Amsterdam. Charles II sent four warships and more than 2,000 soldiers to the Lower Bay to claim the land. The Dutch, with fewer than 150 soldiers, had no

➤ New Amsterdam became a diverse community early in its history. By 1643 more than 18 different languages were spoken in the colony.

➤ On the official seal of the city of New York are beavers, which symbolize the fur trade, and barrels, which symbolize the flour trade. These two products started New York on its path to greatness.

choice but to surrender. New Amsterdam was then immediately renamed New York in honor of the English king's brother.

The port flourished under English rule, as New York became a leading exporter of flour. By the 1670s, New York was conducting trade with other English colonies in North America as well as ports in Europe and the Caribbean. Goods such as paper, ink, and farming tools were routinely imported through the Port of New York. English governor Edmund Andros was instrumental in turning the city into an important center of trade. He was responsible for the building of a new dock and he passed an act forbidding people to throw garbage into the harbor.

In 1664 the Dutch governor Peter Stuyvesant surrendered to English troops and handed over the colony of New Amsterdam, which the new owners renamed New York.

35

A Revolution Begins to Brew

Although England—which became part of the Kingdom of Great Britain in 1707—encouraged the growth of the port, its new trade policies began to infuriate many colonists. To help finance the rising costs of their colonies, the British passed a series of laws that put financial burdens on New Yorkers and other colonists. One law stated that the colonists were not allowed to trade certain items with other countries and could only export them to the British. In addition, goods that the colonists wanted to obtain from other countries could only be imported from Britain. Some New Yorkers reacted by smuggling goods through the port.

Another British law, the Stamp Act of 1765, put a tax on all printed paper items, such as newspapers and even playing cards. The colonists so strongly opposed this law that the British Parliament repealed it the next year. In 1767 the British decided to put a tax on tea and other major imports. New York and the other British colonies reacted by boycotting these taxed goods. New Yorkers were so intent on punishing the British for their severe trade restrictions that by 1768, virtually no imports of British goods came into the Port of New York.

Resistance to the British measures grew in all of the 13 American colonies until 1775, when war broke out. The American Revolution had tremendous consequences for the port. British commander General Howe arrived in New York Harbor with 9,000 troops on June 29, 1776, and the British remained in control of the port from that day until the end of the Revolution. Although the port was closed to commercial trade during this period, it was not totally without

In 1765 large, rowdy crowds gathered in New York to protest the Stamp Act. New York's merchant community was a vocal opponent of Britain's commercial policies.

activity. Military shipping continued down the coast as well as across the Atlantic, as the British moved their troops and military supplies in and out of the port to replenish their soldiers throughout the colonies.

U.S. General George Washington's triumphant entrance into New York in 1783 marked the end of British occupation, which had lasted throughout the American Revolution.

Rebuilding Trade ▶ By the end of the war in 1783, the city of New York—part of the new United States—was nearly in ruins. The port itself was in a terrible state, and the task of rebuilding commerce lay ahead for merchants who wanted to regain their trade contacts across the continent and around the world. The next year, 1784, a small vessel called the *Empress of China* departed from the East River. Commanded by Captain John Green, the ship headed for Asia and the possibilities of renewed international trade. With a cargo including furs and American ginseng (a medicinal herb), the *Empress* arrived in China. This trip was the rebirth of successful international trade for New York merchants.

New York's ascendancy was not without its obstacles, however. Foreign politics sometimes

▶ On April 14, 1789, George Washington was inaugurated in Federal Hall as the president of the United States. New York City became the country's first capital and retained this honor until 1790.

37

affected the port in unfavorable ways. In 1803 Britain and France went to war, and both sides tried to restrict maritime trade by enforcing blockades and intercepting enemy cargo vessels. As a result, both nations began to seize U.S. merchant ships. During this war, the British also forced U.S. sailors into service on British vessels.

In 1807 Thomas Jefferson, the president of the United States at the time, sought to protect U.S. ships and to punish Britain and France by passing the Embargo Act. The embargo prevented U.S. ships from dealing in foreign trade. But the only country harmed by this policy was the United States. Business at the Port of New York and other U.S. ports ground to a halt. The embargo resulted in vast unemployment, as company after company went bankrupt due to the lost business from foreign ports. When it became clear to the U.S. government that the act was disastrous for Americans, the embargo was lifted in 1809.

On Schedule

In 1817 the New York-based Black Ball Line made a startling announcement. The shipping company offered regularly scheduled trips between the ports of New York and Liverpool, England. On the morning of January 5, 1818, the *James Monroe* set sail for Liverpool with eight passengers and a cargo of flour, cotton, and apples. These packet ships, as they were called, started a revolution in sailing. Shipping companies normally had to delay departure until their vessels were filled with cargo or until the weather was conducive to sailing. With the creation of the packet ship, merchants who pre-

▶ In 1807 Robert Fulton, a portrait painter and inventor, designed the first commercial steamboat, the *Clermont*. The vessel traveled up and down the Hudson River from New York Harbor to Albany.

▶ DeWitt Clinton, the governor of New York, initiated the Erie Canal project. Workers broke ground for the canal in 1817 and finished the project in 1825.

The punctuality of New York's packet ships enabled New York merchants to capture the most lucrative and desirable cargoes from traders who could not promise exact sailing times.

viously were not sure when their cargo would depart or arrive could now promise their customers on foreign shores a specific date for the arrival of their merchandise.

Packet lines greatly increased New York's popularity with foreign and domestic shippers as a responsible, efficient port. Packet service also led to the creation of the cotton triangle. With their ability to promise exact shipping dates, New York merchants convinced southern planters to ship their cotton to the Port of New York, where it was unloaded for a fee and placed on vessels headed for Britain. On their return voyages the packet ships would bring back British manufactured goods, which the New York merchants would then have shipped to southern ports.

The opening of the Erie Canal in 1825 also played a significant role in the rise of the port. Covering more than 350 miles from Albany to Buffalo, the canal linked the Hudson River to Lake Erie on the western border of New York. Before the canal was built, travel to the lands that border the

The Erie Canal was the first important national waterway in the United States. Horses and mules on shore towed canal boats through the waterway, which was 363 miles long and four feet deep.

Great Lakes was difficult and time consuming. To reach these areas from Albany, travelers had to brave an arduous trip by stagecoach over the Appalachian Mountains. The cost of moving goods to and from this region was high. When the canal opened, commerce and travel flourished as the price of transporting goods dropped from $120 to $14 a ton. In addition, the canal shortened the time it took to send merchandise from Buffalo to New York City from 20 days to 8 days.

The canal enabled major exports, such as wheat, oats, corn, and other grains, to be transported from farms and factories around the country to the port via canal boats. From there these goods were exported to European countries, as well as to the Caribbean and to South America. The canal also allowed manufactured products from New York City to be sent quickly and cheaply to the Great Lakes states and farther west.

The success of the packet lines and the Erie Canal made New York the primary destination for imported goods and the leading exporter of domestic products. New York

▶ The "peep o'day boys" were New York merchants who arose at dawn to see if any of their ships had appeared in the Narrows.

▶ By the 1860s, more than one-third of U.S. exports and more than two-thirds of U.S. imports passed through the Port of New York.

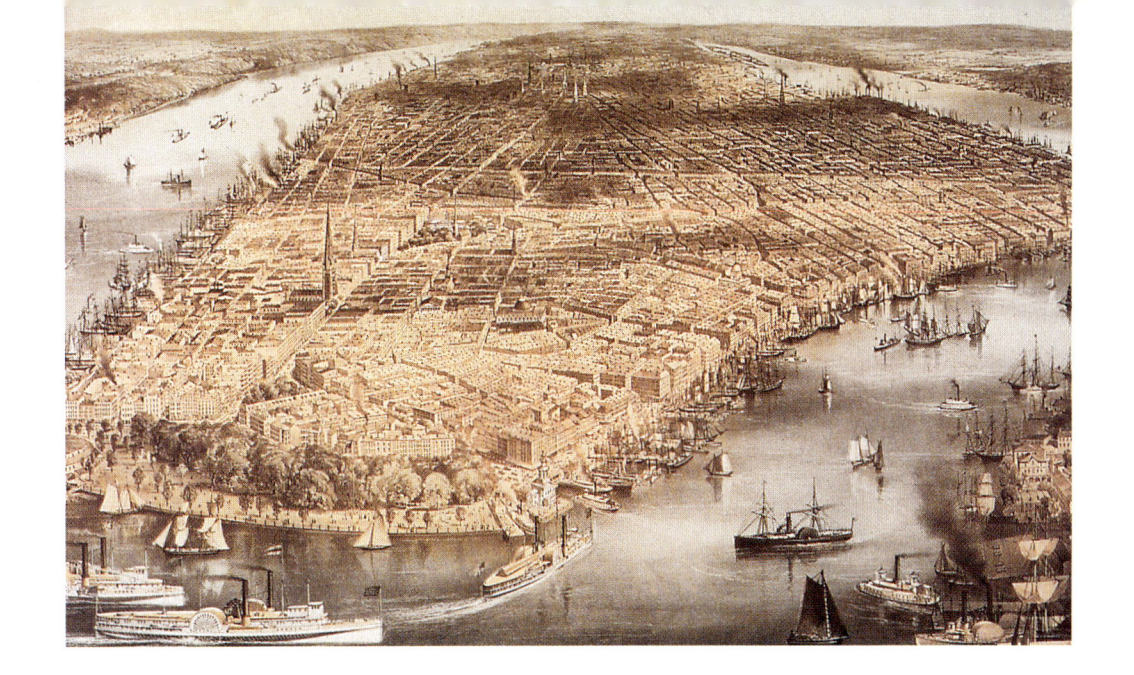

In the 1800s, the port spurred the economic growth that helped New York City become the country's center of trade, finance, and manufacturing.

merchants accumulated great wealth, and the city began to emerge as a center of finance. At the same time, the steam engine, which enabled the production of items in mass quantities, was ushering in the age of manufacturing in New York. By the middle of the 1800s, hundreds of manufacturers in the city were producing goods for both foreign and domestic markets. The garment, leather, and furniture industries all flourished during this period.

Shipbuilding was another significant industry at this time. The port had always been known for producing sailing vessels, but between 1844 and 1854, shipyards along the East River produced some of the finest clipper ships in the world. These vessels were notable because they sacrificed cargo space to achieve greater speed. Money that was lost because of less cargo space was made up by quicker voyages. Clipper ships became especially popular as a result of the California gold rush of 1848.

The ships carried fortune seekers from New York City around Cape Horn in South America all the way to San Francisco.

The center of all the shipping activity was South Street, located on the East River at the lower end of Manhattan. Sailing vessels preferred docking on the East River because it was sheltered from strong winds. South Street bustled with the activity of dockworkers, sailors, and passengers. Across from the docks, South Street was lined with the offices of New York's most prominent merchants.

The Age of Immigration

In the late 1800s, the port city gained another resource—new inhabitants and the cultures they brought from abroad. In the first half of the century, New York had welcomed many European immigrants, most notably people from Ireland and Germany. As a result, by 1850 more than half of all New Yorkers in the city were foreign born. During the 1880s, an even greater wave of immigrants came to New York's shores. Most of these immigrants were from Italy and countries in Eastern Europe. Financial woes in the south of Italy and the persecution of Jewish people in Russia and Poland accounted for some of the people who booked passage to the United States. With the huge influx of people, Manhattan's population doubled.

To help handle this wave of people, an immigrant-processing station was built in 1892 on Ellis Island, a small expanse of land in the Upper Bay. On the day that the station opened, close to 700 immigrants passed through its halls with hopes of a better, untroubled life. More than 400,000 people landed on Ellis Is-

> ➤ In 1898 city officials united Brooklyn, Queens, Staten Island, The Bronx, and Manhattan as the City of Greater New York. Workers built subways, bridges, and tunnels to facilitate travel among the boroughs.

Before they could enter New York City, immigrants had to pass through the immigrant-processing station on Ellis Island (right). *The Statue of Liberty* (below), *completed in 1886, welcomed the newcomers to the United States.*

land in its first year. By the time it closed in 1924, 12 million immigrants had come to the United States through Ellis Island.

At the beginning of the 1900s, New York was known as the most important port in the world. In addition to being a major destination for international cargo vessels, it was also a leading passenger port. At the Chelsea Piers on the West Side of Manhattan, travelers boarded immense ocean liners bound for Europe and other foreign ports. But the port also saw a great deal of change during this period. The steamboat had completely replaced sailing vessels as the primary form of maritime transportation, and the majority of port activity had moved to piers on the Hudson River and in Brooklyn.

World War I (1914–1918) increased maritime activity at the port. When more than 2 million

43

U.S. soldiers were shipped to Europe to fight in the war, most of them left from the Port of New York. However, the city's port facilities were badly strained by all of the wartime activity. With port facilities in need of upgrading, the Port of New York Authority was created in 1921 to promote and protect bistate commerce. This organization was run jointly by New York and New Jersey.

In 1941, prompted by Japan's attack on Pearl Harbor, Hawaii, the United States entered World War II (1939–1945). During the global conflict, one-third of all U.S. military supplies and one-half of the nation's troops were shipped through New York to overseas war zones. The Brooklyn Navy Yard was also busy during this period, as workers built and repaired a variety of vessels, including French and British battleships, for the war effort.

The ocean liner Lusitania *made its first appearance in New York Harbor in 1907. The entrance of ocean liners into the harbor was a major event that was accompanied by great fanfare.*

The Rise of Containerization

The advent of containers transformed shipping and the port. Before containerization, unloading and reloading a ship took 10 to 12 days.

In the 1950s, containerization changed the face of the port. Before the invention of containers, breakbulk merchandise had to be loaded and unloaded package by package, a manual process that took many days. Containers, however, could be quickly forwarded to trains or trucks without being unpacked and could be unloaded in a fraction of the time it took to unload breakbulk cargo.

But New York needed a greater amount of open space to accommodate the large containers. In addition, the piers along the Hudson River were not big enough for the large cranes needed to handle container cargo. No one was going to suggest tearing down skyscrapers in Manhattan to fill this need, so the port expanded to the open spaces across the Hudson

Although the port does not see the amount of shipping traffic that it once did, sea trade is still an essential component of New York City's economy.

River in New Jersey. The port's first container terminal opened in 1962 at the Elizabeth-Port Authority Marine Terminal.

Since the advent of containerization, much of the port's commerce has taken place at terminals in New Jersey, Brooklyn, and Staten Island. Although the amount of waterborne traffic has decreased, the port is still bustling with activity. The Port Authority of New York and New Jersey has overseen the transformation of the port, creating and developing new cargo and passenger facilities in New Jersey, Brooklyn, Manhattan, and Staten Island. In addition to port facilities, the Port Authority manages much of the region's transportation network, including the three airports. The Port Authority also owns and operates the World Trade Center, which houses a wide range of businesses involved in international trade and commerce.

The port has undergone many changes, but it is still the number-one port on the East Coast of the United States and a prime gateway to domestic and international markets. The days of the packet lines and clipper ships may be over, but the port is as busy as ever.

A PORT PERSONALITY

One of the most important persons in the history of the Port of New York and New Jersey, Frank O. Braynard has a colorful history of his own. A resident of Sea Cliff, a town on the shores of Long Island, New York, Mr. Braynard is a maritime author and illustrator. He has written 6 volumes on the *Leviathan*, the largest ship in the world during the World War I era, as well as 39 other books on ships and shipping. He has been the curator of the American Merchant Marine Museum in Kings Point, New York, since 1972.

Mr. Braynard organized OpSail, an event that brings tall ships and other historic vessels from all over the world to New York Harbor in celebration of the Fourth of July. The first event was held in conjunction with the New York World's Fair of 1964. The second, in 1976, brought 175 vessels to the port to celebrate the nation's 200th anniversary. In 1986 the third gathering commemorated the 100th anniversary of the Statue of Liberty, and in 1992, OpSail was held in honor of the 500th anniversary of Christopher Columbus' first voyage to the Americas. Another OpSail event is scheduled for the year 2000.

Mr. Braynard also helped with the renovation of the South Street Seaport and the establishment of the museum there. Together with Peter and Norma Stanford, the president and vice president of the museum, Mr. Braynard helped make the South Street Seaport one of the greatest public attractions in New York City. Visitors to the seaport can board historic ships and imagine how, in past centuries, immigrants and precious cargo came through a port that will always be rich in history.

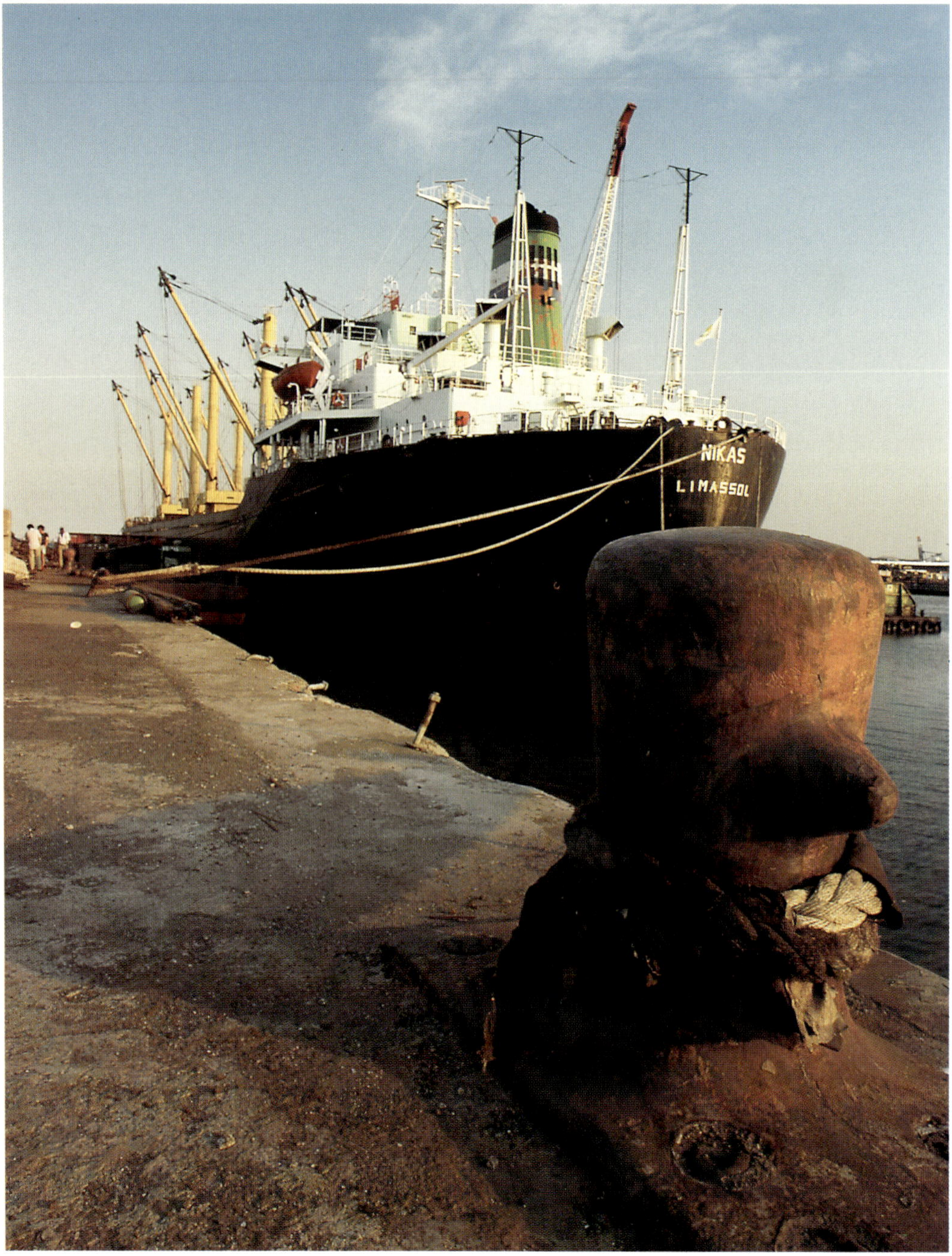
NIKAS
LIMASSOL

CHAPTER THREE

GIVE AND TAKE

A general cargo vessel from Cyprus (facing page) *waits to be unloaded at Port Newark. Ships travel to the Port of New York and New Jersey from nearly 150 different countries.*

If you have three candy bars but no video games, and your best friend has six video games but no candy bars, the two of you may want to become trading partners. Your friend could give you one of her oldest video games (because she is tired of playing it) in exchange for two candy bars (because she's hungry). You may have had too many snacks and wish to trade some of your candy bars in exchange for her video game because you've never played it.

Something within human nature makes us want to give away things that we have in great quantities, and in return, to receive items that we lack and desire. The same principle is also true of international trade, or trade between foreign countries. Many developed nations manufacture items such as computers and automobiles because they possess the money, the machinery, the labor force, and the factories that are needed to produce these items easily and efficiently. However, some developed nations lack raw materials, such as metal ores or wood, that are necessary for the manufacture of certain products. This is where trade comes in. By exporting their manufactured goods to other countries, developed nations make money to buy raw materials from nations with abundant natural resources.

Some countries in South America, Asia, and Africa, for example, can grow coffee beans, which thrive in warm climates. However, these countries may lack the means to produce certain items, such as cars or other manufactured goods, because they don't have the factories to produce them. So these countries export their coffee beans in order to obtain money to import manufactured goods from industrialized nations such as the United States.

The comparison of the value of a country's imports and exports is known as the **balance of trade.** When a country earns more money from its exports than it spends on imports, that country has a positive balance of trade. On the other hand, nations that import more than they earn from exports have a negative balance of trade.

The Port of New York and New Jersey is a major hub of international shipping because it is the largest regional marketplace (in terms of population) in the United States. More important, it continues to be a gateway to markets in

◀ **International and Domestic Trade**

> ▶ The total value of cargo handled by the port in 1996 was $66.4 billion.
>
> ▶ In 1996 the Port of New York and New Jersey was responsible for 15.5 percent of all the water and air trade in the United States.

the midwestern United States and in eastern Canada. In 1996 the port moved 51.3 million long tons of total cargo to international and domestic destinations. The greatest growth was in the area of exports, while the amount of goods shipped from foreign ports decreased.

The amount of imports and exports can fluctuate for many different reasons. For instance, if the winter in the New York area is mild, fewer homeowners will need to buy rock salt to break up ice on their sidewalks, and consequently, the amount of imported rock salt will decrease. If economic activity is booming in countries that trade with the United States, then the rate of exports shipped through New York and other U.S. ports will increase.

A mountain of imported salt, which is used to dissolve ice during the winter months, sits at the Red Hook Container Terminal.

Imported cars fill the lots of the Auto Marine Terminal in New Jersey. The Port of New York and New Jersey is the leading port in the United States for the import and export of automobiles.

One of the most significant trade items at the Port of New York and New Jersey is automobiles. Since the 1950s, when the first shipments of European cars were introduced to the United States, automobile shipping has been big business. The port's numerous automotive terminals handle cars for import and export. Cars made by U.S. manufacturers such as the Ford Motor Company and General Motors are shipped through the port to countries in Europe, South America, and Asia. Cars are also imported from Germany, Japan, South Korea, and Italy to be sold at dealerships throughout the United States. In 1996 the port handled 413,000 automobiles for import and export.

Although cars are the port's highest profile cargo, the number-one general cargo export item is wastepaper, which includes old newspapers and other used paper items. Wastepaper comes to the port from the Midwest,

New England, eastern Canada, and the New York/New Jersey region. Countries such as South Korea, the Philippines, and China purchase this used paper from the United States to produce recycled paper and cardboard. The benefit for these countries, and the world, is that fewer trees are logged for paper. In 1996 the port exported more than 1 million long tons of wastepaper.

In the mid-1990s, other leading general cargo exports out of the Port of New York and New Jersey included plastic materials, lumber, building cement, fruits and nuts, fish and fish products, fresh and frozen vegetables, aluminum, hides and skins, gas and diesel engines, and toys and sporting goods. The top bulk exports were iron and steel scrap, corn, and wheat. Overall, the port's leading export partners include South Korea, the United Kingdom, Indonesia, Germany, the Netherlands, Taiwan, and Brazil.

On the import side, the port's top cargoes are liquid and solid bulk products, with petroleum leading the way. The Port of New York and New Jersey is the number-one importer of petroleum in the United States. In 1996 more than 12.1 million long tons of crude (unrefined) petroleum came into the port from countries in the Middle East. Other major bulk imports included more than 7 million long tons of gasoline, 1.7 million long tons of rock salt, and more than 900,000 long tons of gypsum, a mineral that is a key ingredient in plaster of Paris, which is used to make models, molds, and surgical casts. Leading general cargo imports include automobiles, building materials, fruits and vegetables, clothing, and furniture.

At an anchorage in the Narrows, an oil tanker transfers its cargo onto a barge.

Although the port handles more bulk products than general cargo, the dollar value of general cargo, which includes expensive items such as automobiles, is higher than that of bulk goods.

The port's leading general cargo import partner is Germany, which ships automobiles, auto parts, beer, and paper to the port. Another leading import partner is China, a producer of consumer goods such as toys, sporting goods, and footwear. Italy provides the port with construction materials, furniture, and vegetable oils. South American countries such as Brazil and Venezuela ship coffee beans and bananas to the port. Other top import trade partners are France, Japan, the Netherlands, the United Kingdom, Ecuador, and Saudi Arabia.

➤ Europe is the port's number-one regional trading partner, followed by South America, Asia, and the Middle East.

➤ The Port Authority has several overseas offices that work to develop trade with Europe, Asia, Africa, and other parts of the world.

At Port Newark, a worker inspects the outside of a liquid bulk tank. These large tanks can hold a variety of products, such as petroleum, vegetable oils, and orange juice concentrate.

A SWEET SHIPMENT

Africa is an ocean away from the United States, but every time you bite into a scrumptious chocolate bar, you are tasting a product of plants grown in African countries such as Ghana and Côte d'Ivoire. Cacao beans, the main raw ingredient in chocolate, are seeds taken from the pods of cacao trees. These tropical plants can only grow in hot climates near the equator. When the cacao pods ripen, workers pick them and remove the beans, which are then dried and shipped to factories that process and manufacture chocolate.

On a cold winter's day, the Danish ship *Freya,* owned by Torm Lines, arrives at the American Stevedoring docks at the Red Hook Container Terminal in Brooklyn. The vessel is carrying 100-pound sacks of cacao beans from Africa. Huge gantry cranes take the cargo off the ship, and port workers deliver it to an immense warehouse at the terminal.

Later the sacks are loaded onto trucks headed for chocolate manufacturers such as the Hershey Foods Corporation in Pennsylvania. Workers at Hershey Foods roast the beans, remove their outer coating, and grind them up in large machines. Other ingredients—such as condensed milk, sugar, and cocoa butter—are added to make milk chocolate. The mixture goes through steel rollers to be smoothed out. Then the chocolate is placed into molds to be shaped into bars or other kinds of candy.

When the candy is ready, trucks ship it to supermarkets and candy stores all over the country. You buy it, and with each bite, you enjoy a sweet taste made possible by African sunshine and American manufacturing.

As one of 300 ports of entry in the United States, the Port of New York and New Jersey is a place where foreign goods can enter the country legally. The U.S. Customs Service imposes customs duties, or import taxes, on all foreign goods shipped into the port. One of the advantages of the Port of New York and New Jersey for foreign shippers is the existence of **foreign trade zones** where importers can store, assemble, and exhibit goods in order to avoid paying regular customs duties. For example, a nation can ship perfume in bulk to a foreign trade zone, bottle and label the perfume there, and pay a lower customs duty. If the perfume were already labeled and bottled when it arrived at the port, the importer would have to pay the higher duty, and consumers would end up paying a higher price on the imported item.

The Port of New York and New Jersey also carries on domestic trade, or trade with other locations in the United States. The port ships local manufacturers' construction materials and refuse by barge to other U.S. ports. In addition, cargoes such as fuel oils and medicaments are shipped to and from U.S. territories in the Caribbean, such as the U.S. Virgin Islands and Puerto Rico. Barges carry petroleum and container cargo from the port to other destinations on the Atlantic coast.

> ▶ More than 12 million people live in the vicinity of the port, forming a highly profitable consumer market.
>
> ▶ The Port of New York and New Jersey has 17 foreign trade zones. Some of these zones are in the port, others are as far away as Buffalo, New York.

Products go through a vast network to get to their final destination. In order to ship a product to a foreign destination, the shipper (the company that makes or owns the product) must go through a series of steps. Before sending export goods to the port, the shipper pre-

◀ **From Seller to Buyer**

56

Because New York's landfills are running out of room, the city's garbage has to be shipped by barge to other states with landfill space.

pares a bill of lading—a contract between the shipper and the motor carrier (a truck or rail company) to deliver the cargo to the port at an agreed-upon time. The bill of lading lists the number of packages, the weight of each package, and the destination. It also includes a description of the goods to be shipped.

For quick and efficient delivery, shippers rely on the services of freight forwarding companies. The responsibility of the freight forwarder is to find the most suitable shipping line and the lowest rates for the shipper. For example, a freight forwarder will locate a refrigerated ship for perishable items such as meat or produce. Once a shipping line has been found for the product, the freight forwarder provides the contracted motor carrier with the name of the vessel, the pier number, and the sailing date. Freight forwarders also obtain dock receipts, which have to be presented to the terminal operator. Once the cargo has been cleared by the terminal operator, the motor carrier delivers the cargo to the dock, where it is unloaded and placed on a ship.

When handling import items, freight forwarders act as customs brokers, processing the paperwork for getting the cargo through customs and arranging for the pickup of cargo by truck or train. More than 600 freight forwarders and customs brokers serve the port.

In the world of international trade, businesspeople known as wholesalers and retailers help a producer or importer move goods to the consumer. New York City has one of the largest wholesale grocery businesses in the country. Grocery wholesalers buy items, such as fruits and vegetables, that are shipped into the port, then sell these items to supermarkets and other retail grocery stores. Finally, the retail stores sell their goods to customers. So when you buy Venezuelan bananas from a grocery store in New York City, you represent the final stop of a long journey.

Trade Regulations and Commerce

Although international trade is a vital component of a nation's economy, it can often cause problems. Many industrialized nations have difficulty adjusting to competition from developing nations, whose imports are often cheaper. As a result, countries sometimes impose trade regulations to protect their own industries from foreign competition. Governments do this by placing **tariffs** on imported goods to protect local industries that produce the same items. Because the tariff makes the imported item more expensive, consumers will often choose to purchase the less expensive domestic item. A **quota** is another type of trade regulation that limits the amount of imports or exports of certain types of merchandise.

> Under NAFTA, tariffs on most goods produced and sold in North America are to be gradually eliminated by the year 2010.

> In 1995 the World Trade Organization (WTO) was set up to administer GATT and to reduce barriers to trade in services and in other areas not covered by the agreement.

The practice of creating trade regulations, known as **protectionism,** is common in international trade. Many nations argue, however, that the removal of trade regulations through international treaties will help economies grow. One example of such a treaty is the General Agreement on Tariffs and Trade (GATT), a treaty that was signed in 1948 by more than 90 nations. Among the treaty's goals is the reduction of tariffs and the creation of a code of conduct for international trade.

Another example is the North American Free Trade Agreement (NAFTA), which went into effect on January 1, 1994. Under this treaty, the United States, Mexico, and Canada are gradually merging into one immense market of close to 400 million people, representing $6.5 trillion of goods and services per year. The objective of NAFTA is to gradually reduce tariffs on goods that are imported and exported among the three North American countries. The United States hopes that NAFTA will result in more trade among the three countries, and thus create more business for U.S. ports. Some people in the United States, however, argue that NAFTA will result in a loss of U.S. jobs, due to increased Mexican imports and to the relocation of U.S. manufacturers to Mexico, where labor costs are lower.

Financial Exchanges > The U.S. economy is a capitalist system, where the means of production and distribution are privately owned and operated for profit. This system is also known as free enterprise, because trade takes place in free markets among many buyers and sellers. These free markets can be large regions, such as states, and can include the exchange of different products, such as food and clothing. The markets can also be financial, where people borrow or lend money. In countries such as China, on the other hand, the government runs the economy. This is known as a centrally planned economy.

New York City provides a great example of free trade at work. While the port deals in the physical trading of goods among nations, financial institutions in New York City handle trade that doesn't take place at the port. An example of this type of trade can be found at the New York Stock Exchange, located in the city's financial district. Stocks are shares in the ownership of a corporation. When a person buys shares in a company, he or she receives stock certificates that entitle the owner to a percentage of the company. When the company is doing good business, the value of its stock is high. Investors can earn money by buying stock at a low price and selling it at a high price. Investors trade millions of stock shares every day at the New York Stock Exchange.

The financial district of New York City is also home to the New York Mercantile Exchange, one of the largest commodities exchanges in the world. A commodities exchange is a kind of central marketplace for buyers and sellers of minerals and agricultural products. Gold, silver, platinum, and copper are all traded at the New York Mercantile Exchange, in addition to commodities such as crude oil, gasoline, heating oil, wheat, and corn. Brokers at the exchange trade these commodities with buyers and sellers all over the world. The goods that are traded, as

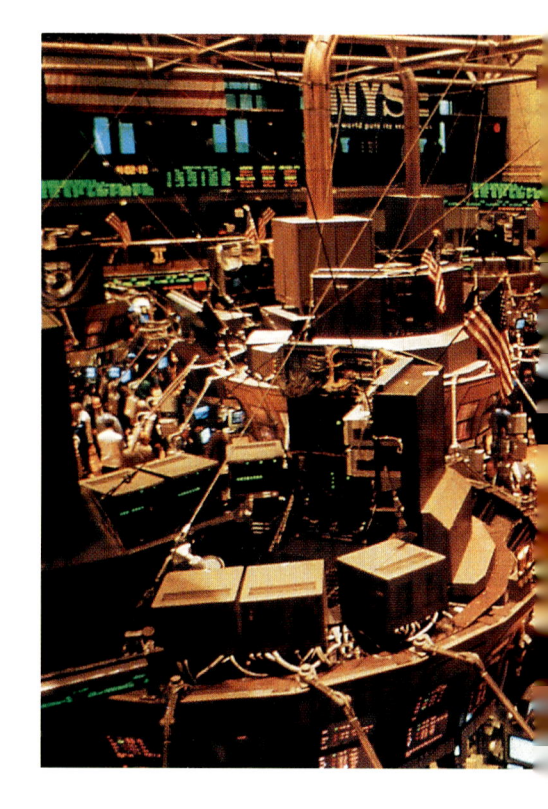

A typical day at the New York Stock Exchange is a flurry of activity, as traders buy and sell stocks for investors from all over the world.

well as the buyers and sellers, are not physically present at the exchange. Transactions are conducted instead through futures contracts. These documents hold the owner of the contract legally responsible to buy or sell a certain commodity at a specific date in the future for an agreed-upon price.

Individuals can buy or sell futures contracts by placing their orders with brokers, who relay the orders to the floor brokers at the exchange. Prices fluctuate according to supply and demand. For example, if there are more sellers of a commodity than buyers, prices will go down. However, if there is a great demand for a product and only a limited supply, people will generally be willing to pay more because the demand is greater than the availability of the good.

Transactions that occur on commodities exchanges affect prices for the retail goods that consumers in the United States and abroad eventually buy. The exchanges and other trade-related businesses in New York make the city the financial pulse of the United States. Whatever happens to business and trading in New York City can have far-reaching effects around the country and the world.

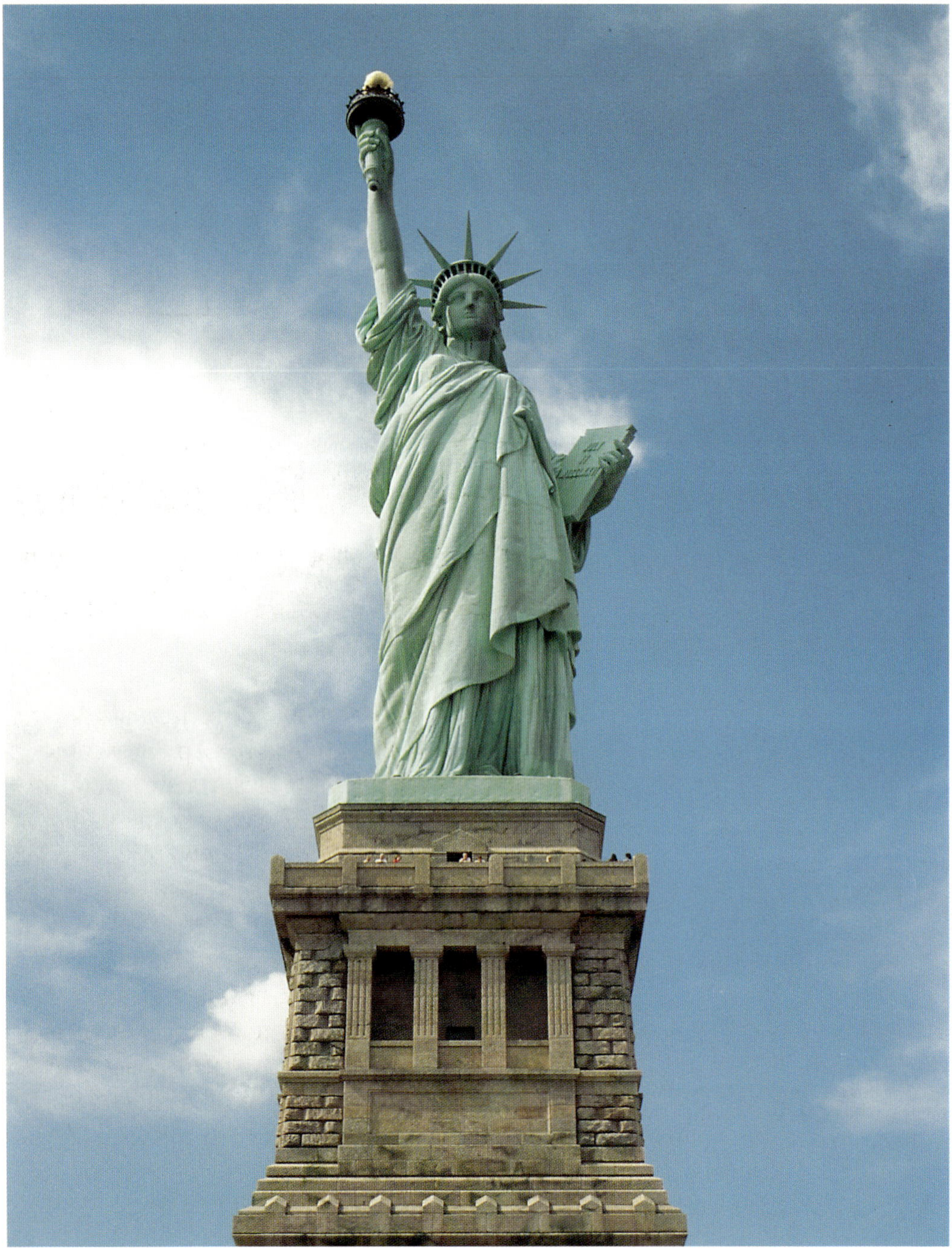

CHAPTER FOUR

THE BIG APPLE

One of New York City's most enduring symbols, the Statue of Liberty (facing page) *has welcomed immigrants for more than 100 years. The statue was a gift to the United States from the people of France.*

In the 1930s, African American jazz musicians dubbed New York City the Big Apple because it represented the ultimate destination for a successful entertainer. The name is still used to refer to a great city that holds a wide appeal for a variety of people and businesses.

New York City has always attracted people from foreign countries looking to settle in a new land with great economic promise. The lure of the port city began with the establishment of New Amsterdam, which started out as a colony with a highly mixed population. In the early 1900s, more than 40 percent of the city's residents came from other countries. By the mid-1990s, almost 90 percent of New Yorkers were foreign born.

New York City's international tradition is still alive. The city's population is 7.3 million people. Included in this figure are a large number of immigrants from the Caribbean, Asia, and Latin America, as well as the largest African American and Jewish communities in the United States. White residents make up 43 percent of New York City's population, while African Americans represent 25 percent of the population. Another 24 percent of the city's inhabitants are Hispanic. Although New York's Spanish-speaking residents represent a number of Latin American countries, people from Puerto Rico make up almost half of this group. Asians account for 7 percent of the population. Native Americans and a variety of other smaller ethnic groups make up only 1 percent of the city's inhabitants.

Although foreign-born New Yorkers live in all five boroughs, some neighborhoods in New York City are famous for their concentrations of ethnic groups. Little Italy is an area in downtown Manhattan that is filled with Italian restaurants, gift shops, pastry shops, and food stores. Nearby is Chinatown, which features telephone booths in the shape of miniature Chinese pagodas. Greengrocers in Chinatown sell traditional Chinese vegetables such as bok choy, a type of Asian cabbage.

In Queens, the largest borough in New York City, diverse ethnic communities sprang up when the Number 7 subway line began running in 1915. This extension of the longest subway system in the world made it possible for immigrants to reside affordably in Queens while commuting to their workplaces in Manhattan.

▶ New York City is the largest city in the state of New York and the most populous city in the United States.

▶ New York City has always been an ethnic food lover's paradise. In the mid-1990s, the city had 8,805 restaurants, many of them dedicated to international offerings. Strolling through New York's many neighborhoods, a visitor can taste Japanese sushi, Italian lasagna, and Hungarian goulash all in one day.

▶ Queens is the largest borough in New York City, covering 126 square miles. Spreading across 34 square miles, Manhattan is the smallest.

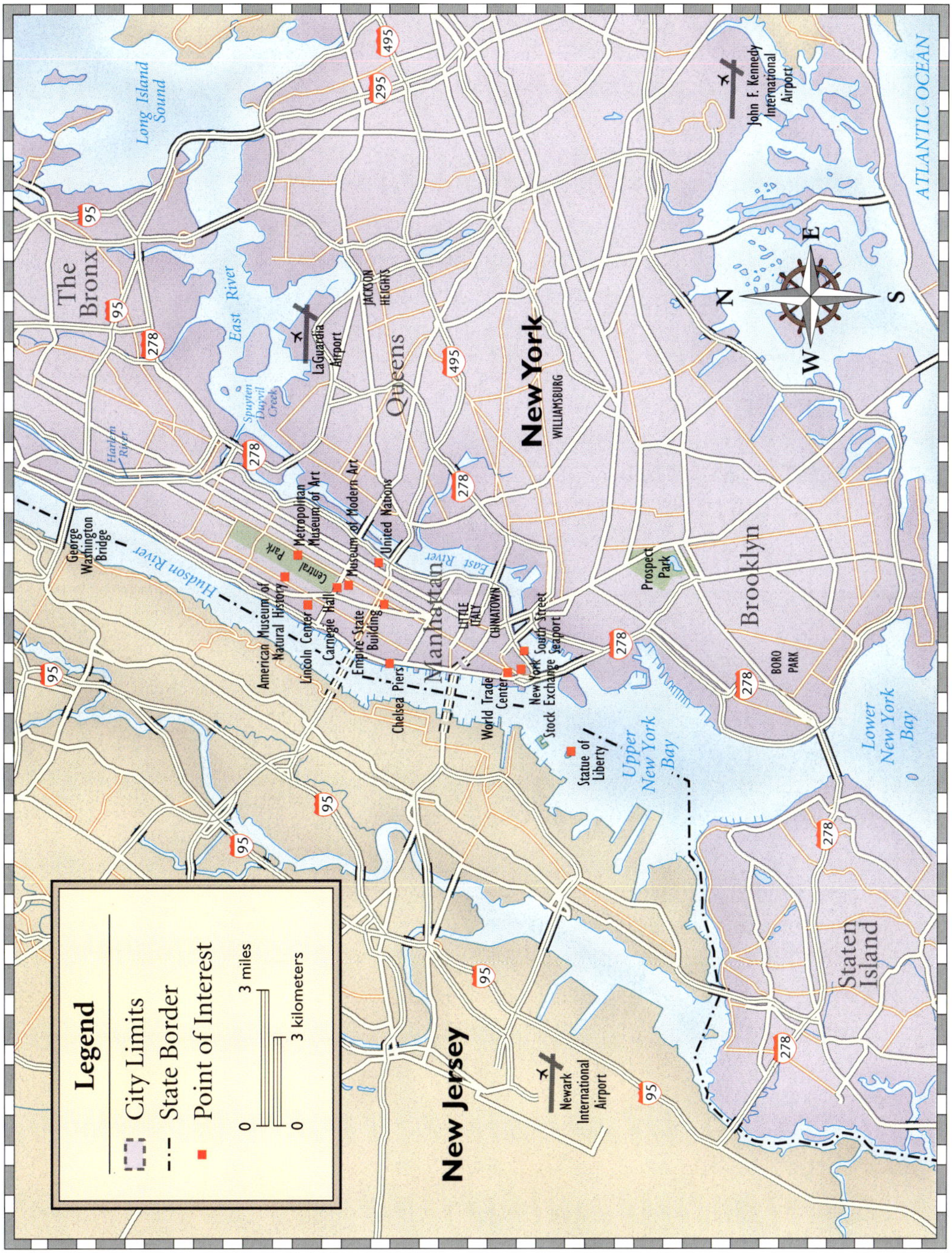

Legend
City Limits
State Border
Point of Interest
0
3 miles
0
3 kilometers
New Jersey
Newark International Airport
New York
WILLIAMSBURG
The Bronx
Queens
Manhattan
Brooklyn
Staten Island
Long Island Sound
East River
Spuyten Duyvil Creek
Harlem River
Hudson River
Upper New York Bay
Lower New York Bay
ATLANTIC OCEAN
LaGuardia Airport
John F. Kennedy International Airport
JACKSON HEIGHTS
George Washington Bridge
Central Park
Metropolitan Museum of Art
Museum of Modern Art
United Nations
American Museum of Natural History
Lincoln Center
Carnegie Hall
Empire State Building
Chelsea Piers
LITTLE ITALY
CHINATOWN
World Trade Center
New York Stock Exchange
South Street Seaport
Statue of Liberty
Prospect Park
BORO PARK
95
278
295
495
N
E
S
W

Because so many different nationalities live along this line, the number 7 train is often called the International Express.

An East Indian section in Jackson Heights, Queens, is filled with stores that sell saris—the traditional dress of Indian women—and restaurants that sell tempting, spicy fare. Farther on along the subway line, you can find Latin American communities with Argentine, Colombian, Ecuadorean, Mexican, and Peruvian restaurants. Many international delicacies are available in the borough's Middle Eastern eateries and Turkish, Greek, and Korean groceries. Filipino, Afghani, and Thai food stores, as well as a Romanian nightclub, are also located in Queens.

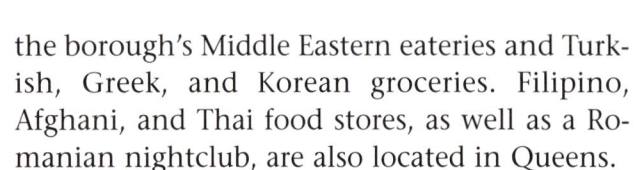

New York City's other boroughs have a variety of ethnic neighborhoods too. Little Odessa in Brighton Beach, Brooklyn, is home to thousands of Russian immigrants. Visitors to the local vodka bars, coffeehouses, and restaurants can enjoy a type of Russian pancake called blini, which is eaten with caviar (fish eggs).

In Queens (above), *Manhattan* (left), *and Brooklyn* (below), *people from different cultures have made their mark.*

> With more than 2 million residents, Brooklyn has more people than any other borough in New York City. If Brooklyn were an independent city, it would be one of the largest in the nation.

Brooklyn also has New York's largest Jewish population. In Jewish neighborhoods such as Crown Heights, Williamsburg, and Boro Park, visitors can listen to the lively sounds of clarinet players performing Klezmer music, which was brought to the United States from Jewish ghettos in Eastern Europe.

Many festivals and celebrations in New York City tie in to events that originated abroad. The Saint Patrick's Day Parade, for example, brings out the luck of the Irish in Manhattan, and Caribbean Americans put on a dazzling yearly parade on Eastern Parkway in Brooklyn to celebrate Mardi Gras—a celebration that precedes Lent, a period of fasting before Easter.

Finance and Culture ➤ New York City has long been a leading center of finance, fashion, the arts, advertising, and telecommunications. Manhattan is the home of corporate headquarters for many major foreign and domestic industrial companies. The New York Stock Exchange—the largest stock exchange in the United States—is located on Wall Street, at the southern tip of Manhattan Island. In addition, New York City's banks are among the most prominent in the world.

The New York Stock Exchange traces its origins back to 1792, when brokers transacted stock sales under a buttonwood tree on Wall Street.

The city's entertainment industry is legendary as well. Major television and radio stations broadcast from New York. People around the world have enjoyed Broadway shows, the New York City Ballet and the Metropolitan Opera at Lincoln Center, and concerts at Carnegie Hall. New York City is also known for its wonderful museums, which include the Metropolitan Museum of Art, the American Museum of Natural History, and the Museum of Modern Art.

A city of many nationalities, New York is also home to the United Nations, an international organization established in 1945 to promote world peace. Other great city landmarks, such as the Empire State Building, the World Trade Center, the Statue of Liberty, and the Brooklyn Bridge, are famous throughout the world.

When many people think of New York City, they think of skyscrapers and sidewalks. But the city has more than 100 parks throughout the five boroughs. The most famous is Central Park

▶ For news, entertainment, and information, New Yorkers can choose among five daily newspapers, six local television stations, and more than thirty local radio stations.

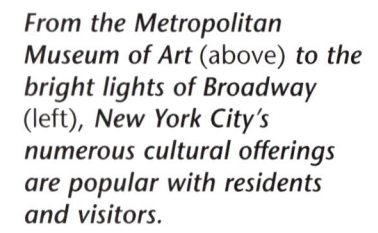

From the Metropolitan Museum of Art (above) *to the bright lights of Broadway* (left), *New York City's numerous cultural offerings are popular with residents and visitors.*

in Manhattan, with its athletic fields, gardens, playgrounds, and wooded areas. Other major parks include Van Cortland Park in the Bronx and Prospect Park in Brooklyn.

The Bethesda Fountain in New York's Central Park is a familiar gathering spot for people and performers.

The Invisible Port ▶ With most of the active areas of the port removed from the lofty skyscrapers of Manhattan and the homes and businesses of the other boroughs, residents sometimes forget that they are living in an active port city. Yet New York City continues to be a marine gateway to the United States for people and products. The city's prominence as a major port still affects the daily lives of everyone living and working in the area of the port.

Jobs at the port and the success of the city's finances are strongly interrelated. When there are more jobs in the area, people have more money for shopping and leisure entertainment.

69

Although Ellis Island is no longer an immigrant-processing station, it still welcomes thousands of visitors each year. The Ellis Island Immigration Museum, which opened in 1990, has exhibits that include old photographs, clothing, and recordings of immigrants sharing their memories of arriving in a new land.

If the economies of the United States and foreign countries are strong, port activity increases, as does the number of tourists spending money in New York City. In 1996 more than 31 million visitors came to the Big Apple, and they spent almost $13 billion.

Many kinds of businesses are directly affected by activities at the port. For instance, the port relies on different companies to carry out the physical handling of goods. Steamship lines own and operate the vessels that transport cargo to and from the port. Stevedoring companies employ workers to load and unload goods on and off cargo ships. Warehouses provide storage space for goods until they are transported by truck or train to their final destinations. These vehicles themselves represent yet another aspect of port business. When merchandise arriving in the port needs to be sent to other cities in the United States, rail and trucking companies move them quickly and efficiently. In addition, the port generates business for bankers who invest in or finance trade and for insurance companies that insure both cargoes and ships.

Some industries in the area are affected by the presence of the port in a different way. If companies need certain raw materials that come in through New York Harbor, they must be situated near the port. Industries such as sugarcane refining and waste materials processing need to be located near the harbor, in order to carry out their business activities without waiting for goods to be delivered from faraway places.

The existence of the port is one reason why residents of the New York metropolitan area—which includes parts of northeastern New Jersey, southern New York State, and southern Connecticut—enjoy lower prices on many items. If goods were imported to other port cities, the cost of additional transportation of these goods by truck or train to the New York metropolitan area would increase the price for New Yorkers.

Directly or indirectly, the port was responsible for over $19 billion worth of sales in the New York metropolitan area in the mid-1990s. Port activities generated 166,500 jobs, resulting in $6.2 billion in wages for employees in the metropolitan region. These wages were in turn responsible for more than half-a-billion dollars of income and sales tax.

The jobs created by the port are part of New York City's large service sector, which employs 90 percent of the city's labor force. People who are employed in the service industry provide a service rather than make a product. Service workers in the city include bankers, waiters,

A vendor offers fresh fish for sale at the Fulton Fish Market, which sells local and imported seafood.

lawyers, government employees, bus drivers and subway conductors, and the people who are employed in the tourist industry.

The other major industry in New York is manufacturing, which employs about 8 percent of the labor force. While the garment and publishing industries are the largest manufacturers in the city, a variety of goods, such as processed foods, electrical machinery, and metal products, are also manufactured in the Big Apple. Construction accounts for 2 percent of the labor force. Workers in this sector build and repair roads and construct new office buildings.

> ▶ New York City is one of the nation's top printing and publishing centers, with more printing plants than any other U.S. city. Almost one-third of the books published in the U.S. are published in the city.

◀ The Future of the Port

In the late 1970s, developers and residents started to view the port not only as a valuable financial resource, but also as an ideal area for waterfront recreation. As a result, the East River—the heart of the port in colonial times—was chosen as the site of the South Street Seaport. Founded in 1967, this 11-square-block area houses buildings with exhibits on the port's maritime past, as well as historic ships such as the *Peking,* built in 1911, and the *Ambrose Lightship,* built in 1908. Other attractions at the seaport include restored buildings from the 1800s, films, lectures, interactive exhibits, and walking tours for children and adults. These programs heighten people's awareness of the port and the city.

The Hudson River has also experienced a rebirth. Because of pressure from environmental groups, this body of water, once highly polluted by industrial waste, is well on its way to regaining its marine life and former natural glory. In 1994 work began on the restoration and mod-

The South Street Seaport (right) *on the East River offers visitors a glimpse of New York's maritime history, while the Chelsea Piers* (below) *on the Hudson River focus on sports and entertainment.*

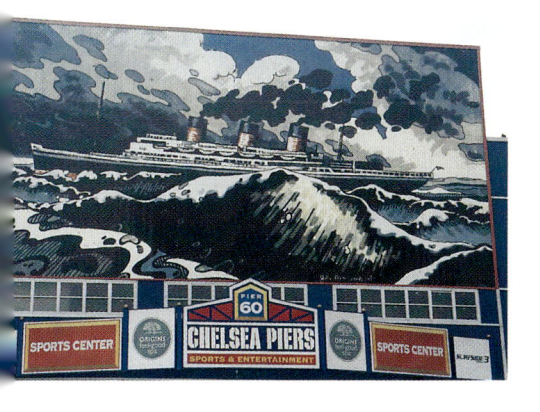

ernization of the Chelsea Piers on the Hudson River. The site has become a modern waterfront sports and entertainment complex that still bears the name of the original structures.

Roller-skating rinks, the only year-round indoor ice-skating rink in Manhattan, a sports center, and a golf course are all part of the complex. Although there are no mountains in the city, the piers feature a rock-climbing wall, basketball and volleyball courts, a boxing center,

73

and a swimming pool. Saunas and steam rooms are available for relaxation after exercise.

The development doesn't stop there. The Chelsea Piers complex is just the first commercial component of what will become the Hudson River Park. In 1997 developers finalized plans for New York City's largest waterfront park, which will one day extend from the southern tip of Manhattan north to 59th Street. The park will encompass 550 acres and include 13 public piers for recreation, environmental education, and arts and entertainment.

Another unique addition to the port city is the New York Water Taxi. Since its beginnings in 1997, the taxi has provided boat service for tourists and commuters heading to local attractions such as the Intrepid Sea-Air-Space Museum, the South Street Seaport, and the Fulton Ferry Landing in Brooklyn.

Waterfront development represents new financial opportunities for the port and the city. As the city enters the twenty-first century, it will continue to experience new growth financially, ethnically, and culturally, just as it did in the early days of New Amsterdam, from which New York has risen to its height as one of the great seaports in the world.

As long as the port continues to modernize and attract new customers, the city of New York will remain a gateway to the United States.

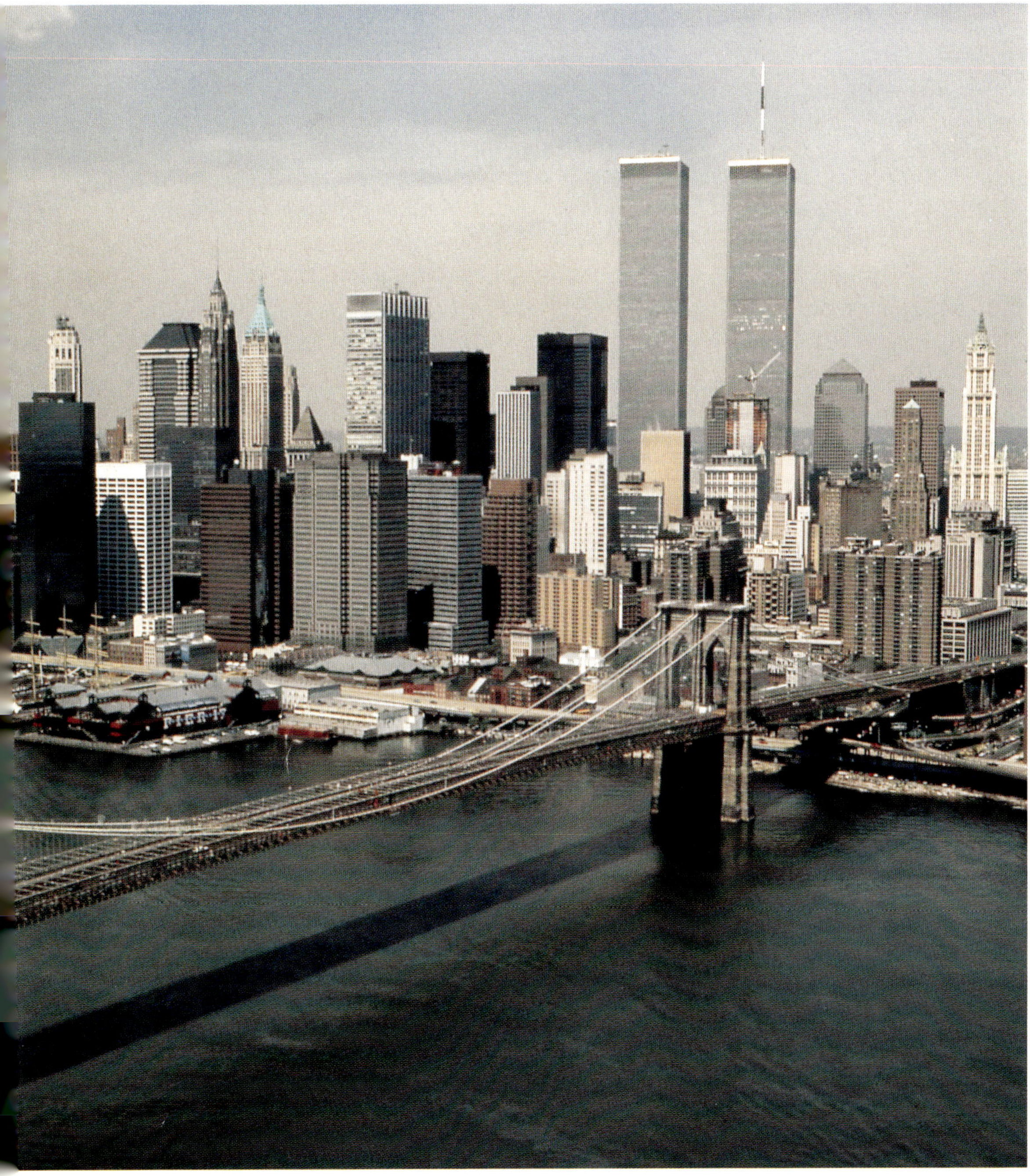

GLOSSARY

balance of trade: The difference over time between the value of a country's imports and its exports.

breakbulk cargo: A term used to refer to non-containerized general cargo. This cargo category includes items packaged in separate units, such as boxes, cases, and pallets, as well as heavy machinery that is too big to be transported in a container.

bulk cargo: Raw products, such as grains and minerals, that are not packaged in separate units. Dry bulk cargo is typically piled loosely in a ship's cargo holds, while liquid bulk cargo is piped into a vessel's storage tanks.

containerization: A shipping method in which a large amount of goods is packed in large standardized **containers**.

dedicated wharf: A docking point for ships used for loading and unloading a specific good, such as automobiles.

foreign (or free) trade zone: An area near a transportation hub such as a seaport or an airport where goods can be imported without paying import taxes. Foreign traders may store, display, assemble, or process goods in these zones before shipping them to places where they will eventually be sold. The United States has about 70 free trade zones.

gantry crane: A crane mounted on a platform supported by a framed structure. The crane runs on parallel tracks so it can span or rise above a ship to load and unload heavy cargo.

general cargo: Cargo that is not shipped in bulk. This category includes containerized and breakbulk cargo.

intermodal transportation: A system of transportation in which goods are moved from one type of vehicle to another, such as from a ship to a train or from a train to a truck, in the course of a single trip.

protectionism: A trade philosophy of protecting a nation's economy by controlling trade with other countries. Countries that protect their markets often allow only certain types of goods into their country.

quota: A limit on the amount of imports and exports of specific goods a nation will accept.

spit: A small point of land extending into a body of water.

strait: A narrow stretch of water that connects two larger bodies of water.

tariff: A tax on imported goods. A specific tariff is applied to each unit of an imported good. An ad-valorem tariff is a tax charged to the importer as a percentage of the price of the good.

TEU: Twenty-foot equivalent unit. Container traffic is measured in TEUs. One TEU represents a container that is 20 feet long, 8 feet wide, and 8.5 or 9.5 feet high.

PRONUNCIATION GUIDE

Brooklyn	BRUK-lin
Bronx	BRAHNKS
Lenape	len-AH-pay
Manhattan	man-HAT-tan
Minuit, Peter	MIN-yoo-it, PEET-ur
Spuyten Duyvil	SPY-ten DIE-vuhl
Stuyvesant, Peter	STY-vuh-suhnt, PEET-ur
Verrazano, Giovanni da	ver-uh-ZAHN-oh, gee-oh-VAHN-ee dah

INDEX

airports, 21–22
Ambrose Channel, 23
Ambrose Light Tower, 22
American Revolution, 36–37
Arthur Kill, 9, 27
Atlantic Ocean, 11–12
Auto Marine Terminal, 18–19, 52
automobiles, 52

balance of trade, 50
Braynard, Frank O., 47
breakbulk cargo, 15, 18, 45
bridges and tunnels, 8, 10, 42
Bronx, the, 8–9, 10, 42, 69
Brooklyn, 8, 10, 12, 18, 42, 43, 46, 66–67, 69
Brooklyn Marine Terminal, 18
Brooklyn Navy Yard, 44
bulk cargo, 14–15, 55

cargo, 14–16, 45–46, 52–54
Chelsea Piers, 73–74
Chinatown, 64
clipper ships, 41–42
containerization, 12, 14–16, 21, 45–46

dredging, 26
Dutch West India Company, 32, 34

East River, 8–9, 12, 33, 34, 37, 42, 72
economy, 59–61, 69–72
Elizabeth-Port Authority Marine Terminal, 17–18, 46

Ellis Island, 10, 42–43, 70
Ellis Island Immigration Museum, 70
environmental concerns, 26–27, 72
Erie Canal, 39–40
exports, 40–41, 50–54
ExpressRail, 20–21

foreign trade zones, 56
future outlook, 72–75

gantry cranes, 15–16
General Agreement on Tariffs and Trade (GATT), 59
Global Marine Terminal, 18
Governor's Island, 10, 24

Harlem River, 9
history, 28–47; American Revolution, 36–37; containerization, 45–47; early settlements, 28–30; Europeans, 31–35; immigration to New York, 42–43; seaport beginnings, 33–35; shipping and trade, 38–42
Howland Hook Marine Terminal, 16, 18–19
Hudson, Henry, 31
Hudson River, 9, 11–12, 19, 26, 31, 32, 39, 43, 45–46, 72–74
Hudson River Park, 74

immigration, 42–44, 62–63
imports, 40–41, 50–55
intermodal transportation, 21

international trade, 49–61

jobs, 69–72

Kill Van Kull, 9, 12

Lake Erie, 8, 39
Lake Ontario, 8
Lenape, the, 30
Liberty Island, 10
Little Italy, 64
Long Island, 9
Long Island Sound, 9
Lower New York Bay, 11–12, 23, 34

Manhattan, 8–10, 12, 19, 42, 64, 67
manufacturing, 40–41, 72
maps, 2, 13, 65
Marine On-Dock Auto Rail Terminal (MODART), 21
Mud Dump Site, 26
museums, 68

Narrows, the, 11–12, 23
New Amsterdam, 32–35
New Jersey, 8–11, 46, 71
New York City: boroughs, 8–9, 42, 64–66; cultural attractions, 68; ethnic diversity, 63–67; financial center, 59–61, 67; history, 7–8, 34–38; population, 64
New York City Passenger Ship Terminal, 19
New York Harbor, 6–8, 11–12, 14, 24–27, 33–34, 36, 47, 71
New York Mercantile Exchange, 60–61

New York Stock Exchange, 60–61, 67
North American Free Trade Agreement (NAFTA), 59

OpSail, 47

packet ships, 38–39
parks, 68–69
petroleum, 53
Port Authority of New York and New Jersey, 14, 46
Port Newark, 17–18
Port of New York and New Jersey: cargo, 14–16, 45–46, 52–54; economic effects on city, 69–72; environmental concerns, 26–27; facilities, 17–19; future outlook, 72–75; inland connections, 19–22; international trade, 49–61; size, 11
protectionism, 59

Queens, 8, 10, 42, 64, 66

railroads. *See* trains
Red Hook Container Terminal, 15, 18, 51
roads and highways, 20–21

Sandy Hook, 12, 22, 24
Sandy Hook Pilots, 22–23
shipbuilding, 32, 41–42
shipping, 12, 14–16, 38–42, 46, 56–58
South Brooklyn Marine Terminal, 18
South Street Seaport, 28–29, 42, 47, 72–73
Spuyten Duyvil Creek, 9
Staten Island, 8–9, 12, 18, 24, 42, 46
Staten Island Ferry, 10
Statue of Liberty, 11, 43, 63, 68
Stuyvesant, Peter, 33–35

tourism, 70

trade, 31–35, 37, 58–59. *See also* International trade
trade regulations, 58–59
trains, 20–21

United States Army Corps of Engineers, 14
United States Coast Guard, 14, 24–25, 27
United States Coast Guard's Vessel Traffic Services, 24
Upper New York Bay, 9–12, 23, 42

Verrazano, Giovanni da, 31
Wall Street, 67
waterfront recreation, 72–74
World Trade Center, 46, 68
World War I, 43–44
World War II, 44

METRIC CONVERSION CHART

WHEN YOU KNOW	MULTIPLY BY	TO FIND
inches	2.54	centimeters
feet	0.3048	meters
miles	1.609	kilometers
square feet	0.0929	square meters
square miles	2.59	square kilometers
acres	0.4047	hectares
pounds	0.454	kilograms
tons	0.9072	metric tons
bushels	0.0352	cubic meters
gallons	3.7854	liters

ABOUT THE AUTHOR

Linda Tagliaferro was born in Brooklyn, but she has also lived in Manhattan, Queens, and Staten Island. Ms. Tagliaferro is a writer and illustrator whose previous book, *Genetic Engineering: Progress or Peril?* was published in Lerner's "Pro/Con" series. She is also working on a book about the Galápagos Islands for Lerner's "Discovery" series. In addition, Linda is a regular contributor to the *New York Times*. Although she has lived in cities around the world, Linda loves New York best because of its international flavor. She has studied Balinese and flamenco dancing in Manhattan and performed East Indian dancing in a Hindu temple in Queens. Linda lives in Little Neck, New York, with her husband and teenage son.

AUTHOR ACKNOWLEDGMENTS

I would like to thank the following people, who helped me with information for this book: Mr. Catucci and Bill Fiumara of American Stevedoring, Inc.; the staff at the American Merchant Marine Academy Library in Kings Point; Norm Goldberg; Mike Scotto; The U.S. Coast Guard; Andrew Miller of the Army Corps of Engineers; the Port Authority of New York and New Jersey; Frank McKenna and Miss Lee of the Douglaston-Little Neck branch of the Queensborough Public Library; Joyce Gold for her superb class on Manhattan history at the New School for Social Research; Frank O. Braynard, curator of the museum at the American Merchant Marine Academy in King's Point; Dr. Stanley Freed of the American Museum of Natural History; Alexander Wood at Big Apple Greeter; Tom Fox of the Fox Group; Dr. Richard Horn of the NAFTA Intermodal Transportation Institute; the Hershey's Food Corporation; and everyone else who made this book possible.

J 917.47 T

Tagliaferro, Linda.

Destination New York /

c1998. (J1

Queens Library

Hillcrest Branch
187-05 Union Turnpike
Flushing, NY 11366
718/454-2786

JUN 3 0 1999

QUEENS BOROUGH PUBLIC LIBRARY
0 1184 7774939 4

FEB

SEP 1 6 1999

MAR 1

OCT 1 9 1999

JUN 2 2

AUG 7

NOV 1 6 1999
DEC 1 8 1999

OCT 11

APR 0

JAN 0 2000

APR 1

JAN 1 0 2000

MAY 0 7

JAN 2 5 2000

JUN 1 4

All items are due on latest date stamped. A c
made for each day, including Sundays and h
that this item is overdue.

Queens Library

OCT 3 0 2001

NOV 1 0 2001

NOV 1 9 2001

DEC 8 2001

JAN 2 6 2002

FEB 0 6 2002

JUN 3 2002

APR 1 7 2003

MAY 1 9 2003

AUG 7 2003

12/30/05

All items are due on latest date stamped. A charge is made for each day, including Sundays and holidays, that this item is overdue.

Rev. 420-1 (4/01)

NO LONGER PROPERTY OF
THE QUEENS LIBRARY
SALE OF THIS ITEM
SUPPORTED THE LIBRARY.